Ch

St. Helens Libraries

Please return / renew this item by the ~~last~~ ~~date~~ ~~sh~~own.
Books may be renewed ~~by~~

KU-545-074

Telephone - (01744) 676~~~~
Email - centrallibrary@sthelens.gov.uk
Online - sthelens.gov.uk/librarycatalogue
Twitter - twitter.com/STHLibraries
Facebook - facebook.com/STHLibraries

WES

THE FASTEST GUN IN TEXAS

Known only as Colorado, he is one of the fastest and most feared guns in Texas — but still falls for a trap while riding across the Panhandle, and is shot and left for dead by thieves who steal his horse. Wounded, he stumbles across an isolated ranch, and is nursed back to health by its owner Helen Blaine. However, the ranch is under the protection of Quanah, a Comanche chief, who forces Colorado to prove his worth by fighting one of his warriors . . .

Books by Edwin Derek
in the Linford Western Library:

ROWDY'S RAIDERS
ROWDY'S RETURN
THE BARFLY
DEAD MAN'S BOOTS
THE AVENGERS OF SAN PEDRO
ACROSS THE RIO GRANDE

EDWIN DEREK

THE FASTEST GUN IN TEXAS

Complete and Unabridged

LINFORD
Leicester

First published in Great Britain in 2014 by
Robert Hale Limited
London

First Linford Edition
published 2017
by arrangement with
Robert Hale
an imprint of The Crowood Press
Wiltshire

*A catalogue record for this book is available
from the British Library.*

ISBN 978–1–4448–3198–6

Published by
F. A. Thorpe (Publishing)
Anstey, Leicestershire

Set by Words & Graphics Ltd.
Anstey, Leicestershire
Printed and bound in Great Britain by
T. J. International Ltd., Padstow, Cornwall

This book is printed on acid-free paper

1

'Joe, where the devil are you? Come here boy, I want you to fetch the sheriff, pronto.'

Joe was the stable boy, no more than thirteen years old. Instead of working, he'd been round the back of the stables practising to draw his six-gun. Of course, it wasn't a real one, just a carved wooden replica, but to Joe it was his most prized possession. His favourite occupation was practising his draw, for he wanted nothing more than to become a gunslinger and be called the fastest gun in Texas like Jake Cobb or the young pretender (and his own particular hero) known only as Colorado.

However, he had learnt that when the boss of the livery stable, Mr Mason, called he'd better come running and damn quickly too. Otherwise, a clip round his ears was the least punishment he could expect. So he took off his holster and, together with his wooden six-gun, hid it in a pile of fresh straw. Then, he raced round to the front of the stable expecting at least a severe reprimand. But Mr Mason had more important things on his mind. Not least of which was the magnificent golden-coloured palomino stallion he was holding by its reins.

'So there you are, boy, playing make believe again, I suppose,' he said angrily.

'No, sir, I was just tidying up round the back,' said Joe, but he looked guilty.

'Never mind that. Go fetch the sheriff, tell him to come here at once.'

'But I'll have to give the sheriff a good reason, he won't come just on my say so,' protested young Joe.

'Use your eyes, boy. Who rides a golden palomino?'

Joe's face went blank, then the penny dropped. 'You don't mean?' he gasped.

'Yes, there's no doubt. It's Colorado's horse. Go get the sheriff. There's a big reward out for the outlaw and your share will be thirteen dollars when he's caught and I get my cut of the reward money. Now go and bring the sheriff straight back.'

Thirteen dollars was a tidy sum for a stable lad who earned only fifty cents a day. His young mind in a turmoil, he raced down Main Street. He covered the two hundred yards or so in record time only to find the sheriff wasn't in his office.

'He's gone to Indian Creek, there's been a shooting. I don't expect him back for a couple of days,' said his deputy abruptly.

'But it can't wait, it's urgent. Mr Mason says there's an outlaw called Colorado in town and he reckons there's a big bounty for his capture.'

The deputy's eyes lit up. Officially, as a law enforcement officer, he could not receive any part of any reward offered for apprehending an outlaw. But there were many ways round the embargo and the deputy knew them all.

'Very well, I'll come with you, but it had better not be a wild goose chase.'

It wasn't. While Mason filled in the

deputy, Joe took the palomino's reins and led the stallion to a stall and then returned to listen to the two conspirators.

'Colorado said he was going to the hotel to get a bath and a meal. Then, I expect a man on the run like him will have a drink or two and find himself a bar room floozy for the night. That should give you the chance to catch him unawares.'

'The hell it does!' exclaimed the deputy. 'The first thing you learn about this job is that top gunslingers like Colorado or Cobb are never taken unawares, even when they are taking a bath or in bed with a floozy. Unlike you or me, their six-guns are always at hand no matter what they are doing.'

'So will you go after him?' asked Mason.

'Of course, but I'd be a damn fool to do so on my own. The sheriff has taken the usual posse members with him to Indian Springs so I'll just round up some good old boys, friends of mine who are not too particular how the job is done, just as long as they get their cut of the bounty.'

'How long will it take to round them up?' asked Mason.

'No telling, but I'll probably be back around about midnight. With any luck Colorado will be in bed with one of the saloon girls by then.'

'For a few dollars I could pay a floozy to make sure that happens,' said Mason.

'That's the first sensible thing you've said. Luckily, I've just been paid,' said the deputy, counting out ten dollars, a quarter of his normal monthly pay. 'Make sure there's some girl with him all night. Get two girls if necessary. Mind, I want my money back, so I'll take it out of your cut of the bounty.'

'What's my cut? asked Mason.

'A quarter for you and the same for me. The rest to be shared equally between the men I'm going to deputize. Now, where's young Joe got to?'

'Here,' said Joe, walking out of the shadows.

'Now listen, Joe. Keep your mouth

shut.' The deputy again delved into his wallet, fished out four dollars and gave them to the boy. 'If any word of this gets out it will be the worse for you and your ma. But do as I say and when we've caught this outlaw I'll match whatever Mr Mason has offered you.'

Joe nodded, his mind full of the promised thirty dollars. Yet that meant betraying his hero and he couldn't do that, or could he? Even though he had never met Colorado, was he, like Judas, going to betray his hero for thirty pieces, even if they were dollars? Whatever he decided he was going to keep the four dollars the deputy had given him. He needed that money to pay the latest doctor's bill. His ma had consumption and she wasn't getting any better.

'Back to work,' ordered Mason. 'You can work an extra couple of hours t onight cleaning the stables to make up for the time you lost playing out the back with that wooden pistol when you should have been working.'

The deputy collected a horse from the stable, saddled up and rode out of town. Mason went back to his office leaving Joe to muck out the stables. It took him much longer than his boss had said it would but he knew it would go badly for him in the morning if he left the work unfinished.

Joe lived with his widowed ma on the edge of town. He daren't ask her what he should do, she was too ill to be bothered by his troubles. However, after bathing under the yard pump and then eating dinner, his mind was made up. He waited until he was sure his ma was asleep and slipped out of his home. It was not quite eleven o'clock. He had to hurry; the deputy had said he might be back around midnight.

But he did not know what Colorado actually looked like so he did a round of the saloons asking for the man who owned a palomino stallion. At the third saloon, he found Colorado ensconced in the arms of an amorous saloon girl. Had she been paid by his boss to keep

Colorado from leaving town? If so, he had to think quickly.

'I have an urgent message from Mr Mason about your palomino. He says you need to come to the stables at once,' he lied.

'Better see what's up but I won't be long,' said Colorado to the floozy as he tossed a dollar on to the bar. 'Barman, pour the lady a drink until I get back.'

The floozy pouted in mock disappointment as Colorado left.

'Now what's this all about and what's a youngster like you doing in a saloon at this time of night?' asked the outlaw as they approached the obviously deserted stables.

'Mr Colorado, my boss recognized you and your palomino, he's called King isn't he? He sent me to get the deputy sheriff but he wouldn't face you alone; he's gone to round up some men. They intend to gun you down tonight while you're in bed. My boss paid that girl you were with to make sure you were in bed with her when they got back. But you must hurry. The deputy will back with his men about midnight and it must be nearly that by now. I couldn't warn you earlier because I had to work late and then I had to wait until my ma was asleep before I could sneak out of the house.'

'But at least you have warned me. So will you saddle King while I get my things from the hotel?'

Joe nodded his head in agreement. Ten minutes later, saddle-bags draped over his shoulder and carrying his specially engraved Winchester carbine, Colorado was back. By then, Joe had saddled King and from the saddle's pommel hung two canteens both full of water.

'Thanks, young man. It's a poor reward for what you've done for me, but here's ten dollars for your trouble. Best put it away for a while. If you start spending it too soon, someone might guess who gave it to you and why.'

'Thank you, Mr Colorado. I'll use it to pay the rest of the doctor's bills; my ma is not too well. She's got consumption.'

'Sorry to hear that, but you might have got a lot more money for her by helping to turn me in. So why are you helping me?'

'Because when I grow up I want to be a famous gunslinger like you.'

The words stung and later on were to come back to haunt Colorado. But now he mounted King and left the town called Evington intending never to return. Yet he didn't urge King into a gallop. At this time of night that might have attracted unwanted attention, so they left at nothing more than a sedate trot. Yet seconds after he had left, the deputy and his cronies rode into Main Street.

Had they rode after Colorado it might have been a close run thing. Before he had retired for the night Mason had deliberately overfed and over-watered King in an attempt to temporarily reduce the palomino's ability to gallop for any distance.

Fortunately for Colorado, the deputy had not seen him leave town. So he and his men cautiously entered the hotel. Finding Colorado's room deserted, they began to search the saloons. By the time they had discovered what had happened it was too late to pick up Colorado's trail. But the deputy sheriff was determined to get the bounty and together with his men, started out at dawn. He was too late, for by then Colorado was long gone and once recovered, no horse was able to outrun King — so much so that three days later when Colorado reined in King, there was no sign of pursuit. As he did so, Joe's words came back to haunt him, *When I grow up I want to be a gunman like you.*

That Joe or any boy should wish to follow in his footsteps troubled him deeply. He had never sought to become one of the most feared gunmen in Texas but had to admit he had earned a fearsome reputation. However, he had no time to dwell on his past. Tired of being on the run, he had a decision to make. There was only one person he trusted to help him decide. Should he visit him? Perhaps, but first he had to ensure he was not being followed.

Colorado was quite certain he had given the deputy sheriff and his posse the slip. So he turned off the main trail on to a little-used back trail, little used because it only led westwards across the Panhandle to a small frontier settlement called Adobe Wells and that was about two hundred miles away.

However, there was a town called Clayton, little more than two days' ride away. There, his old friend, Buffalo Brown, was sheriff. Unfortunately, the town was due north from his present position and as far as he knew there wasn't any trail leading to it. That meant hours of riding through wiry sage brush. Whilst his leather chaps would protect him from the sharpness of their thorns he had no protection for his horse, King. Besides, having lost his trail it was quite possible that the posse would head for Clayton.

Reluctantly Colorado decided against seeking the advice of his old friend and continued along the deserted trail to Adobe Wells. There was no need to hurry, so he slowed King to little more than walking pace.

2

The arrival of the weekly stage in Clayton temporarily broke the boredom of another tedious day, tedious because Sheriff Buffalo Brown's town was as quiet as a graveyard. The reason: the cowhands of both the JB and Lazy K ranches were driving their herds northwards up the Chisholm Trail to Dodge City. It would be many weeks before they returned and already Buffalo was bored to death.

With little else to do, the sheriff studied the passengers as they alighted from the stagecoach. There were three. The first was definitely an easterner, his travel-weary clothes and sample bag marked him out as a whiskey drummer. *There will be no trouble from that quarter*, thought Buffalo disappointedly.

The second man to alight from the stage looked far more prosperous. It was William Dodd, the owner of the town's only hardware store. Middle-aged and more than a little overweight, Dodd had been on a so-called business trip to San Antonio. However, from the self-satisfied expression on his face, Buffalo guessed that at least part of that business had been conducted in one or more of San Antonio's whore-houses. But married to the sanctimonious Mrs Dodd, who could blame him?

It was the last passenger to disembark who most attracted the sheriff's attention. About forty and quite distinguished-looking, he wore a long black jacket, the left side of which bulged slightly. This suggested he was carrying a small, concealed pistol, probably a Derringer. Most people wouldn't have noticed it, but Buffalo's life had often depended on noticing such small details.

Without bidding, Jimmy Jones, the stage's shotgun guard, removed the man's luggage and began to carry it to the town's only hotel. As he did so, the stranger approached Buffalo and introduced himself.

'I'm Eugene Maine from Richmond, Virginia. May I have a word in private?'

Buffalo led the newcomer into his office and gave him a mug of coffee.

'You're a long way from home, Mr Maine. What brings you to my little town?'

'Sheriff, I've been retained to find a man whom I believe might once have been a friend of yours.'

Maine mentioned a name.

'Sorry but you've got the wrong man,' Buffalo said, shaking his head.

'Perhaps you might know him by this.'

Maine pulled out a wanted poster and gave it to Buffalo. Although the sheriff instantly recognized the subject of the poster, he gave no sign of doing so. Instead, he spoke sternly.

'Nothing personal, Mr Maine, I don't cut deals with bounty hunters.'

'Sheriff, I'm a lawyer not a bounty hunter. I've been retained to find your friend and I assure you I'm acting in his best interest.'

'Maybe, and then, maybe not,' replied Buffalo.

'Sheriff, it seems if I'm to enlist your aid, I'll have to take you into my confidence.'

Maine began to explain why his client wanted to locate the outlaw on the poster. By the time he had finished, Buffalo was convinced and struck a deal with the lawyer. Maine was to remain in the town to enable him to conduct some other business. Exactly what that business was, he declined to say. Meanwhile, Buffalo was to search for the man on the wanted poster, a search Buffalo expected to take many weeks, maybe even months, and said so.

'Not a problem,' replied Maine. 'I have leave of absence from my legal firm and as Clayton doesn't seem to possess a full-time lawyer, after I have finished my other business, I'll set up an office and practise law until you return with your friend.'

Early next morning, Buffalo set out. There was no longer a star on his chest. The town had become so quiet his resignation had not come as a surprise to its council. Indeed they welcomed it and the savings it would bring. They had long believed Clayton had been tamed. Therefore, the council had come to believe that they no longer needed the services of a highly paid gunfighter.

As each stride of his horse took Buffalo away from the unrelenting boredom of Clayton, his smile broadened. A former Indian fighter and frontiersman, he was again heading into the wild and vast wilderness of the Texas Panhandle which he considered to be his real home.

Somewhere in the north-west of that great wilderness was Colorado, the out-law whose picture was on the wanted poster. Buffalo had met him some years ago when Colorado had been little more than a callow youth new to the west. Even then Colorado had shown a surprising aptitude with a six-gun. Indeed, when the stagecoach in which they had both been travelling had been attacked by a rogue Apache war party, Colorado had matched Buffalo's not inconsiderable prowess.

Although they remained friends, they had drifted apart. Buffalo had become a lawman and Colorado, although he had never actually broken any law, had been branded an outlaw. He had become so quick on the draw that many believed him to be the most dangerous gunfighter in Texas. Indeed, his reputation as a gunman had spread throughout Texas and some whispered he was even faster than Jake Cobb, previously regarded as the fastest gunfighter in Texas.

However, Buffalo had witnessed both Cobb and Colorado in action and had no doubt who had the faster draw. Not wishing to be drawn into long arguments on the subject, he kept his opinion strictly to himself.

Even in the vast wilderness of the Texas Panhandle, Buffalo had little doubt he would be able to track down his onetime friend. Wherever Colorado went, he invariably sided with the underdog. Indeed, he still sided with settlers and even sod busters against any Yankee ranch owner who threatened them.

Due to the Civil War, many Texas ranches had been cut off from the cattle outlets in the north and so faced ruin. At the end of hostilities many of these large ranches were bought at knock-down prices by Yankee carpetbaggers. And that had led to Colorado becoming an outlaw.

Colorado had been hired to protect some settlers against a ranch owned by a Yankee carpetbagger whose brother just happened to be the local law officer. This unfortunate lawman had tried to gun down Colorado but had been outdrawn in a fair gunfight. Nevertheless, Colorado had been accused of murder and found guilty by a jury hand-picked by the rancher. With Buffalo's help Colorado escaped but at the cost of becoming a wanted man with an ever-increasing price on his head.

Buffalo was so pleased to be searching for his friend — he had very good news for him — that at first he didn't bother to check the trail behind him. If he had done so he might have discovered he was being trailed. Like Buffalo's friend, this man

19

was also a gunman. He always dressed in black and carried two pearl-handled six-guns and a silver-inlaid carbine. On the butt of the carbine was inscribed a sentiment, *Jake Cobb, The fastest gun in Texas.*

That claim was no idle boast as many other gunmen had found out. Nobody, not even Cobb, remembered how many he had outdrawn. Yet he was a wealthy man, the part owner of a huge ranch in east Texas. So he wasn't interested in bounty money. He was driven only by a fanatical obsession to continually prove he was the fastest gunfighter in Texas.

But the man who called himself Colorado had unwittingly become a contender for this title. Jake Cobb had to prove otherwise for, to the wealthy rancher, life wasn't worth living unless everyone believed his was the fastest draw. Knowing this, Maine had already arranged to secretly meet Cobb in Buffalo's town and cut a deal with him. The fanatical gunman was to trail Buffalo until the one time Indian fighter found

Colorado. Then, in front of as many witnesses as could be assembled, Cobb would call out the latest rival to his title, *the fastest gun in Texas.*

3

The hot Texas sun blazed down on the vast expanse of the Panhandle. Even the breeze was hot and the heat haze it caused served only to emphasize the absolute emptiness of the great wilderness.

A lone horseman, riding at little more than walking pace, broke the stillness. As he reached for his canteen, the rider dislodged a scrap of paper from his saddlebag. Unnoticed, it fluttered behind his horse and gradually wafted to the ground. The scrap of paper was part of a wanted notice. Only the top part was left and on it was a single name: *Colorado*. The reward for his capture was a staggering $1,000.

Colorado had no idea that Buffalo Brown was searching for him and that shadowing every move of his old friend rode Jake Cobb. At that moment Colorado's attention was fully focused on the unusual actions of a bald eagle.

High over a rocky outcrop about a quarter of a mile ahead, the bald eagle began to dive, plummeting towards the ground at an astounding speed. But half-way towards its intended victim, the bird of prey suddenly pulled out of its dive and then flew away.

Colorado's palomino horse tossed its head and swished its golden tail. A casual observer might have thought the stallion was just bothered by horse flies. But Colorado knew differently.

'Easy now, King,' he said softly as he patted the horse's neck. 'I know there's someone in those rocks ahead of us, but it isn't an Indian. The only Indians in these parts are Comanche and no Comanche would give himself away by scaring a bald eagle away.'

Colorado resisted the urge to turn his horse round and gallop back down the trail. Since the reward for his capture read *Dead or alive* to do so might invite a bullet in his back.

Instead, he allowed King to continue forward giving no indication he was aware he was riding into danger. On the contrary, he leant forward and began to stroke the neck of his horse. However, this apparently innocent act enabled him to study the ground on either side of the trail without arousing the suspicion of whoever was hidden in the rocks ahead of him.

King trotted by a narrow dry gulch. Running parallel to the trail, its top was partially screened by sagebrush. Colorado grabbed his carbine and then leapt off the palomino. Not a second too soon. A bullet whistled through the air he had just vacated. A second was directed at the ground where he landed. Fortunately, by the time it struck, he was already sliding down the side of the dry gulch.

It was not a big drop, no more than a few feet. Not waiting to brush himself down, Colorado crawled to a spot where the gulch narrowed so much that the sagebrush on the top of each bank formed an unbroken arch above his head.

For the moment, he was safe. But if the unknown rifleman could not see him, Colorado could not see his would-be assailant. Nor could he stay long in the dry gulch for his canteen was still on King's saddle. Although he was partially protected from the hot Texas sun by the sagebrush, without water he couldn't survive for long.

Nevertheless, he had to play a waiting game.

Colorado had one slight advantage over the bushwhacker; formal identification had to be made before he could claim the $1,000 bounty. Therefore, alive or dead, his adversary had to collect Colorado and take him to the nearest sheriff.

Having such a large bounty on his head, it never occurred to Colorado that the reward for his capture was not the reason for the ambush. Yet King's fine saddle was worth at least a hundred dollars and the palomino stallion would almost certainly fetch double that amount at any horse sale. Unfortunately for Colorado, there would be little trouble in selling the stallion; King was still unbranded and the bill of sale which denoted his ownership was in his saddle-bag.

However, none of these facts entered Colorado's mind as King began to pace nervously up and down the trail. It seemed the palomino was looking for him. Colorado whistled softly, instantly reassuring the stallion which ceased pacing and began to graze.

An hour passed and then two. Then King began to neigh again. However, this time it was in answer to the neighing of another horse. Was the bushwhacker approaching at last or was it someone else?

As silently as possible Colorado scrambled up the side of the dry gulch and then lay prone under the sagebrush. His view was still severely limited but he could just make out King a few paces away. He cocked his rifle as another horse came into view. Its rider stopped by the stallion.

'Easy boy, where's your rider?'

To Colorado's amazement it was a woman's voice. He rose to greet her. It was almost the last thing he did. As soon as he stood up, the world seemed to explode and he felt himself falling back into the gulley. As he lapsed into semi-consciousness, he heard the approach of another horse and then he heard voices. This time it was a man's voice and he was laughing as he spoke.

'Betsy, using you as a decoy works every time. That saddle will fetch a good many dollars, and this is as fine a horse as you will ever see.'

'What about its rider?' asked the girl.

Had Colorado not then lapsed into full unconsciousness he would have heard the bushwhacker's dismissive reply. Yet had the man noticed the torn Wanted poster proclaiming a reward of one thousand dollars for the capture of Colorado, dead or alive, still lying on the trail a few paces away, he might have answered differently.

'Leave him be,' he replied instead. 'Even in this desolation, someone might have heard the shot and I don't want to fight over the saddle-bum's horse and saddle.'

The moon was high in the sky when Colorado regained consciousness. The bullet had only grazed his temple but a fraction nearer would have killed him instantly. As it was, apart from a thumping headache, he was fine. However, his shirt was covered in blood.

He retrieved his carbine. There was no sign of the bushwhacker, his female accomplice or King and with the palomino had gone both canteens of water.

Angry at his foolishness, he spoke aloud.

'Colorado, you're nothing but a fool, letting yourself be suckered in by a woman. Well, there's nothing else I can do but walk. Serve me right if I die of thirst before I find help.'

He had been heading to Adobe Wells but the little settlement was still several days' ride away. On foot and without water, he had little hope of reaching it, unless he met someone along the trail. Unfortunately, in this sparsely populated part of Texas, if he met any riders they would be almost certainly Indians. In that case he wouldn't have to worry about any lack of water, for this was Comanche territory.

In south-east Texas and along most of the Mexican border, especially east of the Pecos, the US Cavalry had successfully combated the worst of the Apache threat, but here in the north-west of Texas, the Comanche roamed at will and made short work of any white man they found wandering in what they still considered to be their hunting grounds.

Cowboy boots, with their high arched sole, were made for riding not walking. So before Colorado started out, he took them off and using his bandanna, tied them together. Then he slung them round his neck.

It was not the first time he had done so. There had been several times during his time in the Confederate Army when circumstances had forced him to do without boots. But that had been some years ago and his feet were not as trail-hardened as they once had been. Nevertheless, he walked barefooted along the desert until dawn.

Unfortunately, the trail then became very stony so he was forced to put his riding boots back on. Doing so gave him an idea. Instead of following the trail as it meandered across this part of the Panhandle, he would cut straight through the sagebrush and rely on his rawhide riding chaps to protect his legs from its thorns.

By doing so he could significantly reduce the distance to Adobe Wells. Besides, there was always the chance he might accidentally stumble across a water hole.

There were none. Instead, he found only a clump of sagebrush which gave some shade. He only meant to rest for a little while, but exhausted, fell asleep and slept soundly through the afternoon heat. Doing so may have inadvertently helped him to survive, for as evening approached a cooling breeze sprang up. Nevertheless, when he awoke he was extremely thirsty.

During the time he had been a soldier he had learnt to live rough and how to find his way across unknown lands at night by using the stars as a guide, especially the formation known as the Big

Dipper. So despite his thirst he continued walking until morning came and then successfully hunted and killed a jack rabbit. As he had no means of cooking it he took it with him. Although he continued to search for water there was none to be found. His plight was becoming desperate.

The breeze became a gale and with it came not rain but a violent thunderstorm. A thunderbolt struck the ground only a few hundred paces in front of him. Its impact almost knocked him off his feet. It also kindled a brush fire. Fortunately, he was upwind of the strike so the fire raced away from him.

He stopped to skin and gut the jack rabbit before cooking it in the burning embers left by the raging fire. Although it was badly charred on the outside, he ate every morsel; he hadn't eaten for two days.

Colorado had just finished eating when the rain came. Torrential freezing rain, heavier and colder than he had ever encountered. He took off his Stetson, turned it upside down and placed it on the ground. Within seconds, it began to fill.

The rain lashed down so hard it doused the brush fire. He was soaked to the skin and dangerously cold. Luckily, the wind which had brought the thunderstorm and then the rain also drove them away allowing the sun to reclaim the sky. The temperature rose rapidly. It became so hot, Colorado's clothes seemed to steam as he drank the water that had collected in his upturned Stetson.

He continued walking until, a couple of hours later, he stumbled across a small pool formed by the storm rain and again drank his fill. Then, although he felt bloated, he drank still more; there was no telling when he would find any more water.

But he did. Or, to be exact, the long-horn cattle he began to encounter found it for him. He simply followed their well-worn trail until he came to a water hole and camped there for the night.

★　★　★

Next day, the terrain began to alter. The sagebrush gave way to wiry grass. Dotted here and there were small clumps of cottonwood, too stunted to be called trees. Nevertheless, they provided some shelter from the fierce heat of the afternoon sun, so he rested under them until nightfall. However, lack of food was becoming a problem. Since he had been bushwhacked he had only eaten the jack rabbit he had caught.

It was a clear night. The position of the Big Dipper indicated he had veered too far south. Adobe Wells was now north-west and still several days away. Ahead stretched the Stake Plains. The Comanche, not the white man, commanded this vast and otherwise unpopulated wasteland which stretched westwards for countless miles until it reached the border with New Mexico.

Long past dawn, high in the sky, circling buzzards replaced the lone bald eagle he had seen some days ago. Perhaps their presence was the reason for the lack of any sort of small wildlife. There was nothing for Colorado to hunt.

However, after the fifth night after the bushwhacking, he decided to continue walking until at least noon in the hope he might find something edible to hunt. He didn't. Instead, he stumbled across a small ranch, if ranch was not a too grand a description for the ramshackle house, dilapidated barn and small, broken-down corral. Indeed, he might have missed the little ranch altogether had it not been for the tall, windmill-like water pump which could be seen from afar. Lack of water and food and the unrelenting heat of the mid-day sun had almost taken the last of his strength; it was a struggle to cover the last half mile to the little ranch.

There were many chickens running loose about the place. Perhaps he could buy one? However, his overriding need was water. Yet before he could reach the wind-pump, there came a warning shout from the small ranch house followed by the ominous click of a rifle being cocked.

'What do you want?' asked a female voice.

Framed by the doorway of the house was a young woman holding a rifle. Even in his far-gone condition Colorado could see that she was unusually attractive, nothing like the work-weary women usually to be found living in such isolated terrain. By her side was an odd-looking young lad, about twelve or thirteen years old.

'If I could just have some water, ma'am, and a scrap of food...' He was about to add: 'And then I'll be on my way,' but never got the words out. The heat of the sun and lack of food and water finally overcame him; his carbine clattered to the ground as he pitched forward and fell into unconsciousness.

4

When Colorado eventually came round, he found himself in a soft bed. At first his vision was blurred; nevertheless, he tried to get up only to be restrained by a delightfully feminine hand.

As his eyesight began to clear, he found himself looking into a pair of deep blue eyes belonging to the woman who had threatened him with a rifle. He guessed she was in her early twenties. Her chestnut-coloured hair was long enough to brush against her shoulders. She wore a high-necked white blouse and a long gingham skirt.

'Don't try to move yet, Mr Colorado,' said the woman, blushing as he gazed at her. Nevertheless, she managed to continue in a brusque and business-like manner. 'Yes, I know your name; it's engraved on your rifle. But don't try to look for it. I've locked it away with your six-guns.'

'It's a carbine, Miss, not a rifle.'

Colorado rasped the words in a hoarse voice he barely recognized as his own. 'Whatever,' she replied. 'But it's not Miss. It's Mrs Blaine and you won't get your guns back until my husband returns and decides what's to be done. Until then, I'm not about to let a gunman with your reputation carry six-guns in my house.'

'Fair enough,' croaked Colorado. 'My apologies for calling you Miss. My excuse is that you're not wearing a wedding ring.'

'I always take it off when I do the washing up,' she said rather too hurriedly.

'Fine, but where is Mr Blaine?'

'Not far away. No more talk; eat this broth and then rest.'

He again tried to sit up but found he was as helpless as a newborn kitten.

Seeing his plight, she called to her youngster.

'Leave your chores and give me a hand to prop up Mr Colorado.'

Between them, the youngster and Mrs Blaine managed to prop him up with some extra pillows. Then, she spoon fed him like a baby. The warm broth coursed through his body but instead of reviving him, it made him feel sleepy. So less than an hour after he had awakened, he was again asleep.

However, that was not so surprising, for the broth contained herbs known to induce sleep. They had been left by Isa-Tai, the young yet hugely influential Medicine Man of the Kwahadi-Comanche, although it had been another Indian who had taught her how to use them.

How long he slept, Colorado never knew. Although he had not been embarrassed by being spoon fed like a baby, he most certainly was when he discovered that under the blanket he was completely naked.

Before he could find his clothes, the blue-eyed woman returned carrying the largest mug of coffee he had ever seen. This time, she was wearing a wedding ring although Colorado noted it did not fit as tightly as it ought to have done. The coffee was milky and sweeter than he would normally have liked, yet he drank it and asked for another.

'Of course, Mr Colorado,' Mrs Blaine replied. 'When you've finished it, could you manage a nice juicy steak?'

'Yes,' he croaked. 'You will find some money for it in my clothes, but where are they?'

'In the boiler being washed. They smelt to high heaven and you still do. I'll bathe and clean up your head wound, but for the rest, as soon as you can get up, you can bathe under the water pump. As to your money, it's locked away with your guns. I don't know where you come from but us Texas women don't take money for looking after the wounded, so I'll thank you not to insult me again by offering to pay for food.'

The steak was enormous, yet he had no difficulty in eating all of it and then following it with two helpings of apple pie. After all, it was the first proper meal he had eaten in over a week.

Next day, although still weak, Colorado felt much recovered. However, without his clothes he was not about to leave his sick-bed. But when he asked for them, she refused.

'What's the point of washing them if you are going to wear them still smelling worse than a pig? You can wear some of my husband's old work clothes until you get washed.'

Still naked, Colorado was in no position to argue. So after the aforementioned garments were brought to him by the youngster, he put on the pants and went to shower under the pump. Although the cold water temporarily refreshed him, by the time he returned to the ranch house he was again exhausted.

It took several days for Colorado to recover fully. As soon as she judged him well enough, Mrs Blaine banished him to the barn. However, used to sleeping out in the open with only a saddle for a pillow, the hayloft was luxury by comparison.

During his recuperation, the ranch had no other visitors. Nor did Mrs Blaine's husband return. Indeed, as he convalesced, Colorado noticed several signs of neglect, suggesting her husband had been away for some time. But then, it wasn't really any of his business.

However, getting his guns back was. Unfortunately, Mrs Blaine remained adamant; she would not unlock the gun cupboard until her husband returned. Although he felt defenceless without his Colt, he had little alternative but to wait.

Thus, when on the tenth day of his stay at the ranch visitors arrived, he was unarmed. Perhaps this was just as well since the visitors were a Comanche war party. Armed with the latest repeating rifles and mounted on some of the finest mustangs Colorado had ever seen, they looked to be a formidable fighting force.

While the rest of the war party began to water their horses, their leader dismounted and walked towards the ranch house. He wore a magnificent war bonnet consisting of no less than sixty eagle feathers each tipped with a plume fashioned from the mane of a pure white horse. The Indian's unusual black war paint made him look especially threatening.

Yet his eyes were blue. As far as Colorado knew, no true Comanche had blue eyes, so this one must be part white. Colorado felt a cold shiver of fear run up and down his spine. There was only one Comanche chief who fitted that description, Quanah Parker. He was the most fearsome Indian leader in Texas and third in rank to Bull Bear, the overall chief of the war-like Kwahadi-Comanche.

Back in 1867, most of the nomadic tribes such as Apache, Kiowa, Arapaho and Cheyennes had signed a peace treaty with the white man. One of the exceptions had been one of the Comanche sub-tribes, the Kwahadi.

However, Quanah had not been born a Kwahadi; his father was a young chief of the Nocona, another less fierce Comanche sub-tribe.

Nevertheless, the young Quanah rapidly established himself as an outstanding brave so was allowed to join the Kwahadi.

Among the Comanche sub-tribes, all of whom were taught to ride a horse almost as soon as they could walk, the Kwahadi were acknowledged as the best horsemen and the fiercest braves. Yet even in their renowned company, Quanah's rise had been meteoric.

Now, unarmed, Colorado faced the great Kwahadi sub-chief and attempted to block his path to the ranch house. Then, from somewhere behind him Mrs Blaine called out, surprisingly speaking in Comanche. Quanah stopped in his tracks. His steely blue gaze met that of Colorado. It seemed that the Indian was trying to gauge Colorado's worth.

Mrs Blaine called out again. This time it was a warning to Colorado.

'Stand aside, let Quanah pass. He has come to see me; he will not harm you unless you provoke him.'

Colorado did as he was bid. The great sub-chief walked by him without another glance and strode majestically into the ranch house, quickly followed by an anxious Mrs Blaine. They remained closeted together for about twenty minutes during which time the rest of the braves tended their horses. It was an anxious wait for the unarmed Colorado. Yet when Quanah eventually came out of the house, he strode past Colorado without a second glance, mounted his horse and rode away. The rest of his braves followed him.

As soon as Colorado was certain the Comanche were not going to return, he rushed into the house. He found Mrs Blaine with her arms around her child.

'You have strange friends, Mrs Blaine. Are you all right?'

She didn't answer directly. Instead she spoke to the youngster.

'Go outside and finish your chores.'

The youngster left without speaking, and then to his dismay, Mrs Blaine burst into tears. Not knowing what else to do, he got a cup of water and gave it to her. Awkward though his actions were, they seemed to do the trick. She slowly sipped the water and began to pull herself together.

'What's the problem?' he asked sympathetically.

'Quanah thinks I have a fine boy for

a son, but says he must have a father to teach him how to ride and fight like the Kwahadi. So I must choose one of his braves to marry.'

'Bad enough for you but a Comanche camp is no place for a young white girl,' said Colorado grimly.

Mrs Blaine gasped.

'How long have you known?'

'I've been able to tell the difference even since I was a little boy,' replied Colorado, smiling.

'She's really called Petra. Her pa said she was a tomboy at heart and she has always worn boys' clothes. As we were living out here on our own, I thought it would be safer to continue the pretence.'

'Not when Quanah finds out. You will make him look very foolish in front of his men. To regain face he will almost certainly turn your daughter over to his bucks.

'You know what will happen then.'

'I daren't think,' she admitted. 'But, I'm afraid there's more. I told Quanah that you were my man, so I didn't need anyone else to bring up my child.'

'But what about your husband?'

She didn't answer Colorado's question. Instead, she told him more about the conversation she had with Quanah.

'He said that a man caught without weapons to defend himself is either a brave fool or a coward. For the child's sake he says he must find out which you are.'

'Did he say how?'

'Yes. But luckily, he has been summoned to meet Bull Bear who is very ill. So that must come before anything else. However, when he returns, you must fight one of his braves. If he kills you, the brave will take Petra and me.'

An expression of concern spread across Colorado's face. But the woman who called herself Mrs Blaine misinterpreted its cause.

'Colorado, don't worry. I don't expect you to fight my battles, especially if you aren't allowed to use your six-gun. If you leave now, by the time Quanah returns, you could be miles away.'

'Leaving you and your daughter to face the Kwahadi? I don't think so.'

'No, go. It's not your problem. I'll think of something before Quanah returns.'

'But what about your husband?' asked Colorado again.

She paused before answering nervously.

'I'm afraid I lied to you. I'm not married. Petra is my niece. Her father is my uncle. After my papa died, he moved in. He said it was to protect me. At first I was grateful for the company. Then, he tried to force his intentions on me. When I refused, and I can more than look after myself, he left leaving Petra with me. Luckily, unlike her no-good father, she never stops working. I shall miss her, but I guess I'll have to send her away before Quanah returns.'

'Back to her father?'

'No. I'll cut down some of my old clothes for Petra to wear and take her to a settlement a few days ride from here called Indian Flats. Some good people there I know will look after her.'

'Wouldn't your best bet be to pack up as quickly as you can and then head for Adobe Wells?' asked Colorado.

'Quanah would regard that as a betrayal and would follow us to Adobe Wells.'

'Just over one child? Surely not.'

'Oh yes. Abducting white women and children to take into their tribe is a common Comanche practice. Quanah's mother was white. Yet according to him she enjoyed her life in with the Comanche and married. She had three children, Quanah being the eldest.'

'What happened to his mother?'

'According to Quanah, she was recaptured by the Rangers. But he has always maintained she was taken against her will and has been kept from returning ever since.'

'So what are you going to do?' asked Colorado.

'That's not your problem.'

'I'll be the judge of that. You tended me when I was sick, so I can't leave you to face Quanah on your own. True, I live by my gun, but even a gunfighter has some standards.'

Helen said nothing. Instead, she went to the gun cupboard, unlocked it and retrieved his guns and money.

'It seems I have misjudged you, Colorado. Perhaps you are not as bad as some say you are.'

'I'm no angel ma'am, but I hope I'm not quite as black as some would paint me.'

The evening meal was chicken which the ever practical Petra had killed while Colorado had been in deep conversation with her aunt. Later that evening, after Petra had gone to bed, Colorado made to go to the barn, but Helen stopped him.

'I wouldn't put it past Quanah to leave one of his braves to spy on us. So as you're supposed to be my man, you had better stay in the house. But don't jump to any conclusions; you can sleep in the spare bedroom. I'm grateful for your offer to stay and help me, but not *that* grateful,' she said blushing deeply.

'Ma'am, I'm a different type of man to your uncle. I give you my word; I won't take advantage of the situation.'

'I believe you, Colorado, but you aren't the problem. Anyway, since we are supposed to be a couple, you had better start calling me Helen.'

He couldn't remember the last time he had slept in a bed. Perhaps that's why he was unable to sleep. Instead, he thought about the situation he had gotten himself into. He would stay and fight Indian style. He owed Helen that much, but nothing more. What she chose to do after that was her affair, for he would move on. As long as he remained in Texas, he was a wanted man and the size of the bounty for his capture meant that sooner or later another bounty hunter would be sure to find him.

New Mexico was now his intended destination. Officially, it was a territory not a state of the United States so federal law had no jurisdiction. Wanted notices served in Texas, or any other state, were invalid there. From what he had heard, there was work in Lincoln County for a gunfighter of his undoubted reputation. But this time, he would make sure the law was on his side.

50

There was one other thing troubling him; he couldn't get Helen's words out of his mind: *You are not the problem.* What did she mean by that? He hadn't the faintest idea and eventually fell asleep trying to work it out.

5

It was almost a month before Quanah and his war party returned. By that time, Colorado had not only fully recovered, but good food and hard work meant that he was in the best shape of his life.

The fight was to take place by the windmill pump. Quanah chose his best brave. Colorado removed his six-gun and gave it to Helen. Much to everyone's surprise he also gave her his knife.

'Tell Quanah when I first met him I was unarmed so I'll fight his brave the same way.'

Quanah threw his own hunting knife on to the ground. Through Helen, the fearsome Kwahadi sub-chief indicated that his brave would also fight unarmed. The fight would continue until one of the contestants had been thrown to the ground and was unable to rise. Then, the other contestant would be free to pick up the knife; the combat would continue until one of the combatants was dead.

The rest of the braves formed a loose circle with the knife at its centre. Quanah made Helen stand on his right side and Petra on his left. Standing so close to her, he must have realized she was a girl, but if he did, he gave no indication of doing so.

The rest of the braves were in a good mood. Clearly they thought their brave would win. From the look of anguish on Helen's face, it was clear she thought so too.

Arms extended out in front of him, the Kwahadi brave caught hold of Colorado's hands. But it was only a feint. Without releasing Colorado's hands, the brave locked his right leg behind his opponent's left knee and then pushed hard. Amid the cheers of the other braves, Colorado crashed to the ground, the Indian on top of him.

Half-stunned and with all the breath apparently knocked out of him, Colorado remained motionless on the ground. The brave broke away, scrambled to his feet and looked inquiringly at Quanah who pointed towards his knife. The brave raced to retrieve it.

However, instead of returning to the attack, the brave paused in the centre of the circle, basking in the admiration of his fellow braves. Then, knife raised, he slowly approached Colorado, who, by that time, had regained his feet. However, he still appeared to be struggling to regain his breath.

It looked bad for Colorado; Helen tried to reach Petra to prevent her seeing what she believed to be the inevitable bloody end of the fight. But Quanah stopped her.

'Boy watches! Learn big lesson,' he said, smiling grimly.

Helen translated for Petra's benefit. Then, like a moth to a flame, her attention was drawn back to the fight. Confident of victory, the brave approached Colorado and lunged viciously at the apparently stricken gunfighter.

Without moving his feet, Colorado swayed to one side so the brave's knife missed him by the merest fraction.

Unfortunately for the brave, his forward lunge momentarily caused him to lose his balance.

That moment was all Colorado needed. In a wrestling move too quick for the eye to follow, he grabbed the Indian's knife wrist, and then pivoted. Using the brave's own forward momentum, he threw the Indian over his shoulder. In later years the move was to become known in wrestling circles as the Irish Whip.

However, he did not let go of his grip on the Indian. As the hapless brave flew through the air, Colorado viciously twisted his opponent's wrist. The sound was like the snapping of a dry twig. As the Indian crashed to the ground, Colorado released his grip, turned round and faced Helen and Quanah. She was amazed to see that he had the Indian's knife in his hand. The fight was over; the brave's wrist was broken.

Not the slightest bit out of breath, his earlier apparent difficulty having been feigned, Colorado casually walked over to Helen and gave the knife to her.

'Give the knife back to Quanah,' he said, 'then tell him any young Apache squaw would have put up a better fight. Next time, to make it a more even fight, he had better send for some Apache warriors. Make sure the rest of his braves hear that and understand you.'

Apache warriors. There could have been no greater insult to the assembled Kwahadi-Comanche. The Apache had been the sworn enemy of the Comanche nation long before the white man came to America. But instead of retaliating to the insult, the rest of the braves, humiliated by the easy defeat of their champion, turned away. Without a word, they mounted their mustangs and rode off, leaving the injured brave to mount his steed as best as he could.

Quanah looked Colorado in the eye but spoke only to Helen. Then he took his lance, bedecked with his own colours and thrust it into the earth. Without a glance at the stricken brave, he mounted his horse and rode swiftly after his braves.

'Quanah said that you have proved to

be a warrior worthy to bring up my child and have saved him much embarrassment as he now realizes she is a girl dressed in boy's clothes. He also said you showed great wisdom in not slaying his man. That last bit, I don't understand,' said Helen.

Colorado smiled and then explained.

'Comanche, Apache, Mandan, Crow, whatever their other differences, the nomadic warrior tribes of the Prairies have one thing in common, a strict code of honour.

'With the help of their medicine man, the brave's arm will heal. But it will be some time before he will be able to ride in their war party again. So each time the braves return to their camp, he will be there, living with the squaws. That will be a constant reminder of his defeat and their shame.'

'How did you beat the brave so easily?' she asked.

'Know your enemy. The Kwahadi learn to ride and care for their horses almost as soon as they can walk. On horseback, they are more than a match for the US

Cavalry even when outnumbered by two-to-one. But on foot or in hand-to-hand combat, the Kwahadi are usually considered to be inferior to the Apache. And it was a tough old Apache fighter, called Buffalo Brown, who taught me how to Indian wrestle.'

Colorado was covered in dust, so Helen insisted he washed under the pump. However, now that he was sure that Petra was a young girl, he kept his clothes on. It was also an easy way to wash them; they soon dried in the heat of the Texas sun.

In celebration of his victory, Helen made an extra special effort for the evening meal — steak followed by another of her excellent apple pies.

After Petra had gone to bed and Helen was sure she was asleep, she asked the first of several questions that had been on her mind.

'What do you think will happen next?'

'I believe Quanah's lance means that you and Petra are under his protection. Of course, that protection will only last as long as he remains chief.'

Helen changed the subject. However, not yet daring to discuss what was really on her mind, she asked him what he intended to do next.

'Well since your uncle doesn't look like returning anytime soon, I'll shoe your horses and with Petra's help, finish off the jobs I've started round the place. Then, I must move on. A man who lives by the gun makes enemies and I don't want to bring bloodshed to your home. Besides, young Petra might get the wrong idea if I stay too long. Which reminds me, with Quanah gone, there's no need to keep pretending I'm your man. I'll move out to the barn.'

As she replied, Helen blushed slightly.

'No. I've known Quanah since I was a child. It's just possible he might decide to leave some braves nearby to keep an eye on us. Besides, whatever else they say about you, you're a gentleman. You haven't made one pass at me since you started sleeping in the house and I appreciate that. But as I said before, you're not the problem.'

Colorado still didn't understand what she meant by that. However, before he could ask, somewhat breathlessly, she continued.

'But you're right about one thing, the time has come for me to stop pretending.'

As Colorado turned in for the night, he again pondered her words, *you're not the problem*. What had she been pretending? As before, he tried to work out what she had meant and failed. He was about to give up and go to sleep when there was a knock on his bedroom door. Without waiting for an answer, Helen entered.

Startled by her appearance, he was wide awake in a second. Her long, chestnut coloured hair was no longer gathered tightly in a bun. Instead it once again fell loosely on to her shoulders. The cut of her white nightgown was daringly low and it was so short; it revealed most of her long and very shapely legs, something even the most provocative saloon girls didn't normally do.

'Well, as I said, no more pretending, but will I pass?' she asked anxiously.

'You look fantastic,' Colorado gasped.

'I hoped you'd think so,' she said, blushing profusely. 'It's taken me a long time to pluck up enough courage to wear this in front of you. But enough is enough. Give me a few minutes to change, then follow me; I've something else I want to show you.'

After a few minutes had ticked slowly by, Colorado strode to her bedroom. The door was ajar so he walked in. Helen was sitting on her bed, her discarded nightgown strewn across the floor. She was quite naked. As she pulled him down on top of her, he realized at last what she had meant when she said that he was not the problem.

Next morning, Colorado awoke to find he was alone. The smell of bacon wafting into Helen's bedroom suggested she was already cooking breakfast. True, he was hungry but he would far rather she was still lying naked by his side. He dressed quickly and then joined her in the kitchen.

'Sleepy head,' she said.

'Sorry, I seem to have overslept.'

'That's hardly surprising, seeing as you made love to me for most of the night. Not that I'm complaining,' she said, blushing deeply.

Before Colorado could respond, Petra, lured by the inviting aroma of the almost cooked breakfast, came into the kitchen. As usual, she had been up since before dawn doing her chores: grooming the horses, milking the cow, feeding the hens and collecting their eggs.

They ate a breakfast, mostly in silence. However, Petra's mischievous glances at her aunt and Colorado suggested that she was aware of their night of passion. But wise beyond her age, she said nothing.

After the excitement of the previous day, things went back to a more orderly routine. Colorado re-shod the homestead's horses. There were six: four to pull the old wagon, Helen's own pony and a very frisky mustang.

During the evening meal, Colorado asked Helen about the mustang.

'Could I borrow it to ride to Adobe Wells? Whoever bushwhacked me might have gone there to sell my horse and if you like, I could make enquiries about your uncle at the same time.'

'If you want,' she said. However, there was a doubtful tone in her voice.

It occurred to Colorado that now they had made love Helen might think he was leaving for good. He sought to reassure her as best he could.

'There's a bounty on my head, so there must come a time when I have to move on. In any case, I have to earn a living and the only way I know how is with this,' he said, patting his six-gun. 'But I won't be leaving yet. It's just that a man with a price on his head needs a good horse and there are few better than King, so I need to get him back. I won't leave you alone out here, you have my word.'

Helen was not completely reassured so, although she agreed to let him borrow the mustang, there was no repeat of their night of passion.

The mustang proved to be willing enough. Quite frisky, but none the worse for that. However, the same could not be said for its uncomfortable saddle. If Helen's uncle had given more than ten dollars for it, he had been robbed.

The countryside between the homestead and Adobe Wells was flat and arid. Colorado rode swiftly until it became too hot for the mustang to continue. So he found what little shade there was and rested, allowing the mustang to graze on any grass it could find.

As soon as the afternoon heat began to subside, he rode on. There was little choice. According to Helen, there was no water on the trail to Adobe Wells and he had only two canteens of water — one for the mustang and one for himself.

Colorado camped overnight in a shallow basin some hundred paces off the trail and ate a cold supper. There was no water, but at least there was some grass for the mustang.

Next morning, just before sun-up, they were on their way again. Colorado had already eaten all the food Helen had packed but more seriously, both canteens were now empty. However, because of his early start, he reached Adobe Wells shortly before noon.

The settlement nestled in the bend of a large river — if settlement was not too grandiose a name for just three large buildings and a few old shacks. An educated man, Colorado correctly guessed the river to be the oddly named South Canadian River. He had no idea why it was so called since the river originated in New Mexico and flowed eastwards across north Texas into the Indian Territories which some had begun to call Oklahoma.

Colorado had a tired and thirsty mustang on his hands so he rode over to the stables only to find he had to pay in advance, one dollar per day, for its keep. A steep price so he took the time to ensure the mustang would be properly cared for. As he looked round, he saw that one horse, a palomino, was tethered well away from the other. It was King, but there was no sign of his saddle or saddle-bags.

Once, he would have forced the man in the stable to tell him who now claimed ownership of King. Then, without asking any more questions, he would have found the horse thief and called him out. After he had outdrawn him, he would have ridden off with King, no doubt with a posse chasing after him. But not now. Something deep inside him had changed. Nevertheless, he was determined to get King back.

6

Apart from the livery stables there were only two other large buildings in Adobe Wells. The first, a two-storey general store, contained rooms to let for those who did not wish to stay in the other building, a saloon.

Colorado made his way over to the saloon. Its dimly lit interior was extremely basic. Of course, there was the usual long bar, but unusually there was no mirror behind it. The windows were narrow and their solid oak shutters were clearly intended to keep out more than the bad weather. There were several tables dotted around the pine floor but most of them were unoccupied. Indeed, apart from the bar-keeper, there were only a few men and one woman in the saloon. Clearly used to strangers, the men ignored him. However, the girl smiled warmly. She was dressed like a typical saloon girl and intercepted Colorado as he walked over to the bar.

'My name is Sadie, care to buy me a drink, stranger?' she asked.

'Why not?' replied Colorado. 'Bartender, a beer for me and whatever the lady usually drinks.'

He paid the man and then guided Sadie to a table where they were unlikely to be overheard. There was plenty of choice. After he had bought her a second drink, he asked about her life and her reason for living in such a remote settlement. This was not just idle conversation for saloon girls generally knew most things that happened and all the gossip in the town in which they lived. Although it was a long shot, he hoped she might be able to identify the man who had stolen King or his female accomplice.

Sadie's own story was not so unusual — ditched by the man she loved after he had got her pregnant. Barely fifteen and rejected by her parents, she started to head west, but the wagon train had only been travelling a few weeks when she miscarried. They left her at a settlement to recover but she had neither money nor friends. With no other way of earning a living, she became a saloon girl.

A few years later, accompanied by a group of like-minded girls, Sadie had joined another wagon train. Their destination had been a new settlement in Arizona called Tombstone. A rich lode of silver had been discovered nearby and that had already drawn a large number of miners to it. So a group of gamblers had financed the wagon train. They intended to set up a large saloon in Tombstone and the girls would work there.

From Adobe Wells, across the Stake Plains to the New Mexican border, the wagon train had been promised an escort by the US Cavalry. Unfortunately, when the wagon train arrived there was no escort available. This was not so surprising for at that time there were less than two thousand US Cavalry troops to cover the whole of the west. Unfortunately, without escort, the wagon train had no alternative, it had to turn back.

Very few single women lived in Adobe Wells. Sadie, seeing that there was little competition, decided to set up in the saloon and persuaded two other girls on the wagon train to join her.

All of which was quite interesting but seemed to have little to do with Colorado. Nevertheless, after buying her yet another drink, he struck pay-dirt.

'Since Betsy found herself a regular man, she's become too stuck up to mix with the likes of me,' Sadie continued. 'But maybe that's no bad thing. There's not much business, so me and my other friend, Ami, take it in turns to work in the saloon.'

At the mention of the name Betsy, Colorado took more interest. It was the name the bushwhacker had called his female accomplice. So, after buying Sadie a fourth drink and another beer for himself, he began to question her about Betsy.

But apart from saying her one-time friend had taken to riding off into the surrounding countryside with her new man, only to reappear several days later with a wad of money or a new horse to sell, Sadie offered little more on the subject. She seemed to have other things on her mind.

After two days on the trail, Colorado needed a hot meal and a bath. He mentioned this to Sadie. For a price, she offered to arrange both and a room for the night. Not at the saloon, but across the road above the general store.

Before he went to the store, Colorado returned to the stables to collect his spare clothes from the mustang's saddle-bag. He also searched for King's saddle and was relieved to find it and his own saddle-bags. Although they were at the back of the stable there were too many people about to search the saddle-bags for King's bill of sale. If it had not been removed, he needed the bill of sale in order to reclaim King. Otherwise he might have to resort to gunplay.

The upper storey of the general stores had three rooms to let. It also provided a bath, at an additional cost, of course.

71

In fact, the burly storekeeper would not let Colorado go to his room until he had bathed. There was nothing unusual in that. Fresh blankets and trail-stained cowboys smelling from long and close connections with their horse were not a good combination.

The bathwater was hot and sweetly scented. There was also provision to shave. The actual cost was an extra dollar, twice the cost of the room for a night, but was well worth it.

The unusually large bedroom contained a double bed, a sizable wardrobe and a small dining table complete with two chairs. There was also a dressing table complete with a mirror. Although everything had seen better days, the room was like a palace compared with most in which he had stayed.

Surprisingly, since there appeared to be no other guests, the table was set for two. The storekeeper's wife brought in a side of roast beef far too big for one, even though Colorado was ravenous. Vegetables followed.

But who was his dining companion to be? Colorado didn't have to wait long to find out. As soon as the storekeeper's wife had finished serving, there was a knock on the door and in came Sadie.

She had abandoned her fancy and revealing saloon dress for a simple blue one that had small white buttons on the front of it. She had opted for a more modest appearance since all but the top one was done up. Also gone was most of her over-thick make up. Her almost blonde hair was neatly swept back and tied in a blue bow. Indeed, if it had not been for the mischievous twinkle in her eye and the bottle of brandy in her hand, it would have been hard to tell that she earned her living as a saloon girl.

'I thought you might like some company with your dinner,' she said demurely. 'The food's on me and I've brought a bottle of real French brandy with me, courtesy of the saloon. Perhaps it will take your mind off Betsy; this afternoon, you seemed more interested in her than me.'

'Please come in,' said Colorado, remembering his manners. 'But you're wrong. I'm not interested in Betsy. It's just that I may have met her and her fellow on the trail. If so, they have something that belongs to me.'

'Your horse,' said Sadie immediately.

'How did you know?' Colorado was taken aback by Sadie's astuteness.

'Don't look so surprised; Betsy has been bragging how her man had won it in a poker game ever since they brought it back to Adobe Wells.'

'And you didn't believe her?' asked Colorado as he carved the beef.

'No. I've been around saloons and gambling tables since I was almost sixteen. So I've gotten to know about poker and the men who play it. Frank doesn't strike me as the type to win an important poker hand — lacks the necessary patience and a mite too flash when he's got a winning hand. Besides, he likes girls too much to spend much time playing poker. Ami fancied him rotten but Betsy hooked Frank first.'

'Frank?'

'I don't know his other name. But take care, he has a short temper and is reckoned by those who know about such things to be pretty fast with a six-gun,' said Sadie.

'Where is he now?' asked Colorado.

'Dunno. A couple of days ago he and Betsy went on another one of their trips, though where they find to go in this god-forsaken wilderness, I don't know!'

Colorado had a shrewd idea, but kept it to himself. Instead, he sought to reassure her.

'Don't worry; I have a plan to get King back, so let's hope it won't come to gunplay.'

'If you try to get your horse back, I'm afraid it will. And don't look for the law to help you because apart from when the Cavalry's around, which ain't often enough for a girl like me to earn a good living, there ain't none.'

Colorado's plan had been to go back to the stable later that night and retrieve King's bill of sale. Then tomorrow, he would go to the stable, produce the bill of sale and claim King.

But Sadie had other ideas how he should spend the night. After the plates had been cleared, she smiled demurely but looked him straight in the eyes.

'There's no pudding,' she said. 'So you will have to make do with me for afters. I'll stay all night if you wish.'

The abruptness of her offer took him by surprise, possibly because he was thinking about going to the stable as soon as she left. And then there was Helen to consider.

Sadie misinterpreted his silence.

'There's no charge. Not even for staying until tomorrow morning. Now, a girl can't say fairer than that, can she?'

Colorado had to agree.

She untied the blue bow in her hair and then shook her head. Her hair cascaded on to her shoulders. Next, she began to undo the buttons on the front of her dress. It didn't take Colorado long to realize she was wearing nothing underneath it. So how could he refuse? His plan to get back King's bill of sale would have to wait until tomorrow night.

Buttons undone, she slipped out of the dress and started to undress him. She was as forward in her love making as she had been verbally when she had first spoken to him. So it didn't take her long to make him forget about Helen, for a little while at least. Eventually, passion exhausted, Colorado fell asleep. But not for long, for Sadie woke him at dawn. There seemed to be no reason until her actions made it clear that their passion of the night had been nothing more than the prelude to what she had in mind for the rest of the morning.

Indeed, it was almost noon before Sadie left. Worn out by love making, Colorado slept for another hour. Then he roused himself and went to find the storekeeper to book the room for another night. Next he walked over to the stable ostensibly to check on his mustang. But really, it was to again check out the stable's layout in preparation for the visit he intended to pay that night.

The stables were surprisingly busy. It seemed they had taken a very large and long overdue delivery of sawn timber earlier that morning; piles of it had been stacked untidily here, there and almost everywhere in the yard in front of the stables. There seemed to be a multitude of people either inspecting or trying to buy timber and they all seemed to want serving at the same time. To add to the confusion, the local undertaker had temporarily taken residence and was busily building coffins. Did he know something that Colorado didn't?

Colorado slipped behind the largest pile of timber and then made his way to the back of the stable. Screened by yet another pile of stacked timber, he located his saddle and saddle-bags and opened them.

Unsurprisingly, they were empty. However, he drew his knife and cut the lining of one of them. Then, it took only a few seconds to locate the bill of sale. He slipped it into his pocket and returned to the front of the stable. Such was the hubbub, nobody noticed him.

Casually, Colorado strolled out of the livery stables. As it was too late for lunch, he headed for the saloon and settled for a beer. He had almost finished it when he was interrupted by the arrival of a flashily dressed cowboy. He wore two six-guns, butt first in their holsters. With him was a woman. She was dressed in exactly the same fashion as the woman he had briefly seen on the trail. Although he had not seen her face, he didn't doubt that she was Betsy.

'Stranger, where did you get your mustang?' said the flashily dressed gunman.

'I don't see that's any of your business,' replied Colorado calmly.

'When it comes from my place, it damn well is!'

It had never occurred to Colorado that the bushwhacker and Helen's uncle might be the same person. So, for the first time in his life, he tried to avoid confrontation, for Petra's sake if not Helen's.

'In that case you must be Helen's uncle. She's worried about you and I guess your girl misses you too.'

'That's none of your business,' snapped Frank.

'Perhaps not. But I've been working at Helen's place for a few weeks and came to collect a few things on her behalf. I had to borrow her mustang because I lost my horse.'

'I don't believe you, cowboy. Do you, Betsy?'

'No. I think he's just a common horse thief.'

Colorado didn't take the bait. Indeed, he remained perfectly calm.

'Betsy, that's a pretty name,' he said politely, 'but I've heard it before. Just before I was bushwhacked on the trail, but I don't suppose you know anything about that?' he said, looking straight at Frank.

'What do you mean?' growled Frank.

'Nothing,' replied Colorado. 'Only that I believe I'm in your debt. Sadie tells me you brought in my horse; he's the palomino in the stable now. I have the bill of sale on me which proves my ownership. So I'll be happy to take him back. You can have the mustang in return.'

A small crowd had followed Frank into the saloon, perhaps to see how Colorado would handle any possible confrontation. However, used to the bullying ways of Frank, only few of them realized Colorado was trying to give Helen's uncle an easy way out. Unfortunately, however, it seemed that Frank had mistaken Colorado for just another saddle-bum and so intended to humiliate him in front of his followers.

'I don't trade with saddle-bums and liars. What do you say about that?'

Still Colorado would not be goaded.

'That you are wise not to do so. However, you've only to return to Helen's place with me to check my story. Why don't you bring Betsy as well, I hear she's fond of riding.'

Colorado's jibe brought a burst of laughter from the crowd. It was common knowledge that during his frequent visits to Adobe Wells Frank had been carrying on with Betsy. It was also common knowledge he had also been trying to get Helen to marry him in order to take over her little ranch. But only to then sell it to the highest bidder.

Unfortunately for Frank, the confrontation was not going the way he had planned. Instead of the stranger backing down, the man was making him look a fool. But Frank wasn't done yet.

'I'll give you one chance. Admit you're a horse thief, give me back the mustang and you can walk out of town.'

'And if I don't?' asked Colorado.

'Then, whether you go for your gun or not, I'll shoot you.'

'Well, it seems you leave me with no alternative,' said Colorado.

Frank completely misunderstood Colorado's meaning, so he smiled and began to relax. But if he believed his threat had made this sassy stranger back down, he was quite wrong.

'So, I'll give you the same chance. Admit you stole my horse and I'll let you walk out of town.'

The crowd gasped. In anticipation of

what they believed would happen next, they dived for cover.

Frank didn't disappoint them. He reached for both his six-guns in the firm belief that their butt-forward position gave him the advantage. It didn't. Before either of his six-guns cleared leather, Colorado's Peacemaker Colt spoke. Its bullet struck Frank's chest and penetrated his heart, killing him instantly.

'Murderer,' screeched Betsy.

'No, your Frank drew first,' said Sadie, who had returned to the saloon to see what all the commotion was about.

'That's right,' said a voice from the crowd, most of whom were beginning to stand up again. 'Frank called him out.'

There was a murmur of agreement. Sadie put her arm around Colorado and together they walked out of the saloon.

'That will cost you another night with me,' she said, grinning mischievously.

This time Colorado didn't have to think about it. He took her arm and smiled. In the event, he didn't have to wait for nightfall. Her love making kept him occupied for the rest of the afternoon and then after dinner long into the night. Not that he complained. Tomorrow, he would have to leave Adobe Wells and, as he had little intention of returning, thought he would probably never see Sadie again. He could not have been more wrong.

Colorado had originally intended to head westwards across to Lincoln County in the New Mexican Territories. But to do that he would first have to cross the Stake Plains. That no longer seemed a good idea with the Kwahadi-Comanche on the loose. Perhaps heading southward to the Rio Grande and the Mexican border might prove to be a better idea. But whichever way he chose, first he had to keep a promise; to return the mustang to Helen. Then, he would have to tell her about the gunfight. He was not looking forward to that, but facing Petra was what he most dreaded.

7

Next morning, Colorado had no difficulty in retrieving his palomino and the mustang. He and King had travelled many trails alone but, even with the mustang for extra company, never one as lonely as the one back to Helen's little ranch. Even getting King and his own saddle back was scant compensation for the task his conscience insisted he had to do.

As they approached the ranch, the mustang whinnied loudly. Perhaps it was the response from Helen's horses that brought her outside, for as he approached she was down by the corral waiting for him.

'Where's Petra?' Colorado asked as he dismounted.

'Something disturbed the hens and scattered them all over the place. She's rounding them up.'

'Helen, I have bad news for you and I am afraid it also affects Petra.'

'Coffee's brewing, come inside and tell me what's happened.'

He did just that. To his surprise she showed little emotion at his news.

'I guess all that's left is to tell Petra and move on,' he said sadly.

'That's your answer is it? Run away, leaving me to deal with a broken-hearted girl,' she said sharply.

'What else can I do?'

'You can stay here and help Petra get over the shock.'

'But once she knows I killed her pa, she will hate me.'

'She won't because you won't tell her. I will tell Petra that her pa has been shot dead, but not by whom.'

And that was the end of the debate. Helen would brook no other course of action. But she hadn't finished with Colorado yet.

'If you want to sleep in the house, get yourself cleaned up. Apart from horses you stink of cheap perfume. It seems your nights in Adobe Wells were even busier than your days!'

This possibility seemed to disturb Helen more than the death of her uncle. So not wishing to incur any more of her wrath, Colorado immediately immersed himself under the pump's cold water. He stayed there until he was sure every trace of Sadie's perfume had been cleansed from his body. Nevertheless, the reception he received over dinner was even chillier than the pump's ice-cold, deep well water.

At first, Petra took the death of her pa badly. But that was only to be expected. Helen put her aversion to Colorado's nights in Adobe Wells to one side and discussed what to do about Petra. They jointly decided it was best to keep her as busy as possible. So apart from her normal chores Petra found herself helping out with work more usually associated with ranch hands. Yet, far from objecting, she seemed to enjoy it. Or perhaps it was just working with Colorado that kept her spirits up.

However, he was shocked to discover that Petra could neither read nor write so offered to help in her education. At first, Helen was doubtful but Colorado soon proved to be an excellent tutor. In fact, his knowledge of mathematics and American history proved to be extensive. When pressed on the point he was forced to admit that he was a graduate of the West Point Military Academy.

Helen knew that almost all West Point's cadets came from well-to-do and influential families. So what had happened to his family and why had he become an outlaw? No matter how much she asked, Colorado would not be drawn on the subject.

During the day, when Petra was not having lessons or doing her normal chores, Colorado taught her how to hunt for jack rabbits and fire a carbine. Of course, she was not yet strong enough to fire while standing upright, so Colorado demonstrated how to fire from a prone position.

Each evening after supper, Colorado gave Petra a history lesson, if lesson was the right description. He imparted knowledge in a series of what might be described as factual accurate adventure stories. He started by telling her stories about Stephen Fuller Austin and Sam Houston and the huge part they had played in the history of Texas and its fight for independence from Mexico. He then went on to explain the reasons why the Lone Star State went on to join the United States.

Petra was fascinated by the account and asked many pertinent questions. From then on Colorado related more and more historical stories. Although the tales often lasted well beyond her normal bedtime, Helen didn't object; she too found the stories fascinating, and they gave Petra something to think about other than the death of her pa.

As the days passed by, Colorado demonstrated aspects of character that Helen had never associated with him. Each morning, Petra was his constant companion as together they began to tackle the neglect of years. Then, each afternoon he took turns with Helen to give more lessons. Helen then began to teach Petra to read and write while he taught her basic mathematics. If Helen had begun to fill the role of Petra's late mother, then Colorado gave Petra the attention her pa never had.

However, in spite of Helen's growing admiration for Colorado, there was no further repetition of her night of passion with him. Although whether this was to do with his shoot-out with her uncle or his nights with Sadie, Helen wasn't telling.

Colorado tried to convince himself that Helen's continued coolness towards him was all for the best. After all, he was a man with a price on his head and sooner or later, he would have to be on his way to the border. But which one? Should he head south to Mexico or continue with his original plan and ride west across the Staked Plains into New Mexico? He was still undecided, perhaps because he hoped against hope that before he left Helen would forgive him. Not that her feelings towards him mattered, or at least that's what he tried to tell himself.

Life settled into a familiar round of work and lessons. Petra was a willing pupil and learnt quickly. However, the peaceful routine was soon interrupted by the arrival of a troop of cavalry led by a very young-looking lieutenant. Not wishing to draw attention to himself, Colorado remained in the house. Petra, still dressed in boy's clothes, stopped repairing the corral fence, fascinated by the appearance of the troopers.

'Be obliged if my men could water their horses and refill their canteens, ma'am,' said the lieutenant.

Helen introduced herself.

'The water is free to anybody who needs it,' she said. 'But may I offer you some coffee?'

'Thank you kindly ma'am, but surely you and your boy aren't alone in this wilderness?'

'No. My husband is in the house; he fought for the South during the Civil War and still gets a mite nervous around blue uniforms.'

'Most Texans fought for the South, Mrs Blaine. But the War's long over and in any case, I have four men in my troop who fought for the Confederacy.'

'In that case, Lieutenant, have your men rest a spell while you come inside and meet my husband.'

Colorado had overheard the conversation just as Helen had intended he should. He smiled ruefully. When Quanah's war party had first visited, she had called Colorado her man, now it seemed she had promoted him to her husband. Surprisingly, he found the idea appealing, yet dismissed the thought as impossible. Nevertheless, he could at least act out the part.

'Good day to you, Mr Blaine,' said the lieutenant as Colorado handed him a cup of freshly brewed coffee.

The sounds of Petra repairing a broken part of the corral filtered into the house.

'That's a fine hard-working boy you have, Mrs Blaine. But you look too young to have a son that old, if you don't mind me saying so.'

The remark was probably intended as a compliment. Or was the young lieutenant fishing for information? Maybe not. *Perhaps the blue uniforms are making me over sensitive*, thought Colorado.

'He's sort of adopted,' replied Helen quickly. 'Both his parents are dead. His mother was killed during an Indian raid some years ago and his father, my uncle, was recently killed in a gunfight.'

While Helen busied herself serving more coffee, the lieutenant took Colorado to one side.

'Mr Blaine, could I have a word with you in private?' he asked. 'I don't want to alarm your wife.'

'I don't have any secrets from my wife,' Colorado replied, playing it as he thought any real husband would.

'Very well. I'm afraid there's trouble brewing. A large party of buffalo hunters are planning to hunt north of Adobe Wells in the Staked Plains.'

'You must stop them at once,' said Helen, returning from the kitchen. 'There's supposed to be a treaty with the Comanche preventing buffalo hunters entering the Staked Plains. If its terms are broken, the Kwahadi will go on the war path and braves from the other Comanche sub-tribes will join them.'

'You seem well informed about the Comanche,' replied the lieutenant. 'But I'm not a politician, just a soldier with orders to provide the buffalo hunters with protection against anyone who tries to stop them hunting.'

'But who is going to protect you against the Comanche?' scoffed Helen.

The lieutenant looked at Helen and smiled.

'Mrs Blaine, I've a crack troop of cavalry outside. Experienced men, some of whom have fought against the Apache. I don't think the Comanche will trouble us too much.'

'Think again, Lieutenant,' interrupted Colorado. 'Believe me, Kwahadi-Comanche live to fight and they outnumber you by almost three-to-one. If that doesn't convince you maybe this will. Most of them are armed with the latest repeating carbines and the rest have shotguns. They will blast your men out of their saddles before they draw their sabres.'

'How do you know this, Mr Blaine?' The lieutenant sounded sceptical.

'Because their war party was here,' snapped Helen.

'And they didn't attack you?' The lieutenant sounded even more dubious.

'I have known their leader since he was a boy. Then, he was a Nocona Comanche.'

Helen pointed to Quanah's lance still standing upright where the great sub-chief had left it.

'As you can see, as long as we stay here we're under his protection.'

'But that hasn't stopped him attacking other homesteads and ranches,' said the lieutenant.

'Perhaps not, but when he visited us, he gave me his word that he and his men would leave us alone as long as we stayed here.'

'And you believed him!' exclaimed the lieutenant incredulously.

'Yes,' replied Helen. 'The Comanche prize honour almost as much as valour. Once Quanah had given his word, we were safe. Besides, he isn't pure Comanche, his mother was white.'

'In that case, there might be some chance he might still be persuaded to take his people to a reservation. Soldier I may be, but I should prefer to avoid bloodshed if I can.'

An hour later, the lieutenant and his troops left. If the lieutenant followed his orders and then ran into the Kwahadi, Colorado didn't think many of his troops would return to tell the tale.

Life soon got back to normal and for the time being they were all too busy to think about the lieutenant and his troops. Gradually, months of neglect were put right and Petra learnt to control the frisky mustang Colorado had borrowed to visit Adobe Wells.

One evening, after Petra had gone to bed, Helen again began to quiz him about his time at Adobe Wells. However, she seemed more interested in how he had spent his nights and who with, rather than the shooting of her uncle.

Although Colorado tried his best to play that part of his visit down, Helen persisted.

'Of course, it doesn't matter to me who you slept with,' she said, at last getting round to the one thing which had troubled her ever since Colorado's return. 'It's just you're the only man I've slept with, so what did she have to offer that I didn't?'

'Nothing, but then sometimes nothing is best,' he answered enigmatically.

'I don't understand.'

'Of course you don't. How could you? Look, Sadie works in a saloon. So I was just another man in a long line of men. By now, she will have forgotten me. There was no commitment and so, no regrets. Well, almost no regrets.'

'Almost no regrets?' she asked quietly.

'Sadie is the only sort of woman a man on the run like me can afford to have. Over the years there have been one or two like her in my life. I don't even remember their names. But you, well if things were different, I wouldn't want to leave here. But I have to.'

The anguish in his voice was so unmistakable Helen could no longer maintain her pose of indifference.

'I suppose you're right,' she admitted grudgingly. 'But be warned, you can't blame a girl for trying to change your mind.'

And try she did. In fact, the next few days were some of the happiest of Colorado's life. But it was only to be a short escape from reality. Wounded and bleeding, the lieutenant returned with what was left of his troop, scarcely half the men he had originally commanded.

Fortunately, the lieutenant's wounds were not as bad as they first appeared and few of his surviving troopers were wounded. While Helen tended his wounds, the lieutenant explained what had happened.

'We found the buffalo hunters. Not difficult, the sound of their buffalo rifles and the smell of dead carcasses carried over the wilderness for miles. So we couldn't miss them. But the trouble was: nor could the Indians! They hit us almost as soon as we rode into the hunters' camp. You two were right in one thing — at least some of the Indians were armed with shotguns. They cut us to ribbons but luckily for us, a group of buffalo hunters had been out scouting and arrived back just as we were about to be slaughtered.'

'What happened then?' asked Colorado.

'We regrouped and with the aid of the buffalo hunters we drove the Indians away. Unfortunately, we were in no position to give chase. Instead, we left the buffalo hunters to bury the dead while we rode back to warn you.'

'Thank you, Lieutenant, but we are in no danger,' replied Helen. 'As I said before, Quanah gave us his word and he will not break it.'

'I don't doubt that, Mrs Blaine, but the buffalo hunters said there were no Comanche bodies amongst the dead Indians. Most of the bodies were either

Kiowa or Arapaho but there were also some Cheyenne.'

'If the other tribes have united, heaven help us!' exclaimed Colorado.

'And the United States Cavalry,' replied the lieutenant grimly. 'The buffalo hunters' chief scout rode after the Indians to see if he could find out more about them and I've sent my best rider to my commanding officer, Colonel McKenzie, to ask for reinforcements. But it will be some weeks before they arrive. So, I'm afraid you must pack up immediately and then we will escort your wagon to Adobe Wells.'

'But Lieutenant, what about the other settlement?' asked Helen.

'What other settlement?'

'Indian Flats, it's about forty miles south-east of here,' replied Helen.

'How many live there?' asked the lieutenant.

'Mr and Mrs Hardgrave, the O'Hara and Kelly families I know. There are a couple of families that have only just moved in, plus some farm workers I don't know. Including the children — about thirty.'

'South-east,' mused the lieutenant, thoughtfully. 'That's almost in the opposite direction to Adobe Wells. Still, they will have to be evacuated for their own safety. There's nothing else to be done. Perhaps you had better stay here until we get back.'

8

In order to warn the settlement at Indian Flats and at the same time provide some protection for Helen's little ranch, the lieutenant split up the few fit troops he still had: three stayed at the ranch while the remainder rode with him. However, much to his annoyance, the lieutenant was unable to leave immediately. Thinking they would not be riding again that day, the troopers had let their thirsty horses drink their fill. As a result, their steeds had become bloated and were in no condition to gallop.

At dawn the following day, the lieutenant and the rest of his troop rode away. Helen's directions were accurate and the troopers found Indian Flats without any problems. The lieutenant lost no time in telling the settlers about the attack on the buffalo hunters and then ordering all the families and farm workers to leave. Surprisingly, there were only a few objectors, but the lieutenant was very persuasive, so after further discussions the objectors change their minds.

Nevertheless, the settlers were not prepared to leave Indian Flats immediately. Instead, they insisted on packing as many of their belongings as they could fit into their wagons. It took so long that they were unable to leave until the following day.

Even then, it was far from the early start the lieutenant had planned as the settlers insisted on burning everything they could not take with them. In spite of the lieutenant's ever-growing impatience and with a column of smoke rising from Indian Flats that could be seen for miles, it was almost noon before they eventually left.

Their progress was hampered by the slowness of the Kelly family's ox-drawn wagon and the mules used as pack animals by some of the farm hands. Consequently, their progress was so slow the occupants of the little wagon train were obliged to spend the night encamped under the stars on the open trail. Fortunately, there was no sign of any Indians, whether Comanche or the mixture of tribes which had earlier attacked the lieutenant.

Again owing to the slowness of the Kellys' ox-drawn wagon it was almost sunset before they reached Helen's ranch. However, their arrival caused Helen an unforeseen problem.

Most of this area of the Lone Star State suffered from near desert conditions. Yet by some unfathomable freak of nature, several separate springs provided Indian Flats with unfailing, year-round natural irrigation. But that water came at a cost. Although suitable for farming, the often boggy nature of the ground bred a particularly malevolent type of parasite that made it impossible to breed cattle.

Helen's ranch had, in her father's time, not only employed ranch hands but produced more cattle than the little ranch could sustain. Although those days were long gone, there were still more steers on the ranch than she could sell in Adobe Wells. So she traded some of her surplus stock with the settlers of Indian Flats. At first, it had been a few dozen head after round-up, but her late Uncle Frank had taken it upon himself to sack the ranch hands.

However, the children of Indian Flats needed milk, so the families living there took it in turn to bring a generous supply of fruit and vegetables in exchange for a milking cow. The cow was returned as soon as its supply of milk had run out and before the parasites had taken hold and replaced by another one. So they knew that Helen was not married. Unfortunately, Trooper Smith heard them gossiping about it.

The former Confederate officer had already overheard Helen call her supposed husband Colorado, and that had aroused his suspicions. Although his duty obliged him to inform his lieutenant, he first went to Colorado, not to confront him but to issue a warning.

'Colorado, we all have things in our past that are best forgotten but sometimes the past has a nasty habit of catching up with us. The chief scout of the buffalo hunters was asking if anyone knew where you were. For what reason I don't know. But we are due to meet him in Adobe Wells. Better keep your eyes open, he's one mean-looking *hombre*.'

Trooper Smith then left and informed the lieutenant about Colorado. This left the lieutenant in a difficult position. So he went to find the outlaw.

'Colorado, as we seem to be facing a serious Indian uprising, my first duty is to get all civilians to safety. To do that, I shall need every able-bodied man I can trust.

'Trooper Smith reported his findings about you as he was duty-bound to do. Fortunately for you, I am under no obligation to place any civilian under arrest unless I am presented with a duly authorized warrant by a Federal Deputy Marshal. But can I trust you?'

'You can rely on me, I give you my word,' said Colorado.

'That's good enough for me,' replied the lieutenant.

'So am I under arrest?' asked Colorado.

'Not yet. Of course, I will have to send a report about you to my superiors. That said, when we reach Adobe Wells I will almost certainly have many urgent and pressings matters to which I must first attend. Unfortunately, Trooper Smith, who might otherwise have reminded me about that report, has a terrible memory. So bad, he seems to have forgotten his real name and that he was once a colonel in the Confederate Army.'

Colorado relaxed as he began to understand the lieutenant's meaning.

'As Adobe Wells has neither a sheriff nor a gaol, I would normally have you confined to your room. But my first priority is dealing with the Comanche, so I expect to find that I will have insufficient troops to do that or to follow you in the event that you escaped.'

'And that won't happen until you tell me that the settlement is safe from any Kwahadi raid,' said Colorado.

'We have an understanding then.' The lieutenant smiled and turned away. Since an early start next morning was essential, he began issuing the necessary orders, the discussion with Colorado already forgotten.

Next morning, breakfast was taken very early. Yet it was still long after dawn before the wagons commenced their journey. Helen's wagon led. At her request, Colorado had roped Quanah's lance vertically to the wagon. From the top of the lance, the Kwahadi sub-chief's distinctive pennant fluttered in the breeze.

Although there were not that many wagons, there were still too few troopers to fully protect them. So, once it was underway, Colorado mounted King and joined the troopers. Yet in spite of his reassuring presence, all the troopers now knew his real identity and a feeling of uneasiness spread amongst them.

It increasingly felt as if they were being shadowed yet there were no signs of any Indians. Aware of the growing tension, the lieutenant urged all possible haste.

Unfortunately, his words were in vain; progress was still pitifully slow and worse was to come. Within an hour of starting, one of the horses pulling the Hardgraves' wagon cast a shoe. After it had been unharnessed, Colorado led it back to Helen's ranch. Of course, before it could be reshod, he had to relight the little forge and wait for it to heat up. So it was well past noon before he returned to the wagon train only to find that progress had still been pitifully slow; the oxen pulling the Kelly wagon were not built for speed.

That night, the lieutenant ordered that no camp fires should be lit; he believed they were too likely to attract attention. So they ate poorly and drank only cold water. The next day passed without incident but progress was still woefully slow and, when they camped that evening, they were little more than halfway to Adobe Wells. That night the lieutenant again forbade the lighting of fires.

Next day the worst fears of the troopers were realized. Seemingly out of nowhere, a Kwahadi war party, about twenty strong, appeared on their right flank. The war party was not the one led by Quanah although the braves were bedecked in the same sinister black war paint. However, they made no attempt to attack. Instead, just out of carbine range and in single file, they silently kept pace with the wagon train as if they were acting as its escort.

'What are they waiting for, why don't they attack?' asked Trooper Smith to anybody who cared to listen. He tried to keep the anxiety out of his voice but failed dismally.

However, the answer to Trooper Smith's question was soon forthcoming. As suddenly and as mysteriously as the first, a second war party appeared, but this time on their left flank, and although they wore war paint, it was red and yellow, not black.

'It's the same band that attacked us!' exclaimed Trooper Smith.

'No doubt about it,' confirmed the lieutenant.

And yet this second war party also failed to attack the wagon train. Instead, they too kept pace with the wagon train, and also rode in single file, just out of carbine range. Both war parties remained on either side of the wagon train all day, yet there was no visible communication between them.

That night, there being no further need for concealment, the lieutenant ordered a fire to be lit. The Indians' war parties remained separate and camped on either side of the wagon train, again each party just beyond carbine range. After dinner, the lieutenant posted guards. Colorado and half of the troopers stood watch over the horses while the rest, together with all the other adult civilian males, guarded the wagons. But still the Indians did not attack.

Colorado was nonplussed, for he knew the Comanche valued horses above all else. Apart from the number of his wives, the wealth of any Comanche brave or chief was measured by the number of horses he possessed. They were even more prized if the horses had been stolen from rival tribes or the US Cavalry.

Another breakfast passed by without incident and the wagon train was allowed to move on with no sign of aggression from the Indians. However, each war party resumed their respective positions on either flank and they remained there until dusk.

At sun-up next morning there was no sign of them. Both war parties had left as mysteriously as they had appeared.

In spite of the children's protests, there were no breaks for food along the trail. As a result, the wagon train reached the comparative safety of Adobe Wells late that afternoon.

Colorado was surprised to see that between the three main buildings, which were each about a hundred yards apart, a large number of tents had been erected. There was also a new and crudely constructed corral full of a curious mixture of mules, burros and ill-assorted horses.

From the largest of the tents came the satisfying aroma of cooking meat. Piles of buffalo hides outside two other tents furthest away from the original settlement indicated their occupants to be the buffalo hunters and suggested that it was buffalo meat Colorado could smell cooking.

In between the large tents and the original settlement buildings were several small tents. Children playing outside a couple of them indicated that settlers from other homesteads had also made their way to Adobe Wells.

The lieutenant halted the little wagon train and then began to allocate tents to the families from Indian Flats. He then spoke to Helen.

'Mrs, or should I say Miss Blaine,' he began.

'It's Miss but why don't you call me Helen?' she interrupted.

'Thank you, er, Helen. As you seem to know more about the Kwahadi-Comanche around here than anyone else, I want you to act as my advisor. Therefore, rather than allocate you a tent, I'm going to ask you to move into one of the rooms above the saloon.'

'I understand they are already occupied,' said Helen, coolly thinking of Sadie and the other saloon girls.

'Don't worry about that, I'll have all the girls moved out and guards will be posted at the bottom of the stairs to prevent anyone who isn't authorized from going upstairs.'

'Who will be using the other bedrooms?'

'During the day I shall use one as my headquarters and dining room. Apart from myself, the only men who will normally be allowed to use the upstairs rooms will be the buffalo hunters' chief scout, Colorado, and of course, you.'

Seeing the surprised look on Helen's face, the lieutenant continued.

'I meant what I said; you are to advise me in all matters concerning Quanah Parker and the Kwahadi Comanche. Most of my men are from east of the Pecos and I'm new to Texas. Therefore, your knowledge may prove vital, so I want you to attend every meeting.'

'Lieutenant, where will you put the saloon girls?'

'There's only three. Two can go above the hardware store where they will cause the least problem. I don't want my men distracted from their duties, especially during the night, begging your pardon, ma'am,' said the lieutenant, embarrassed by the direction in which the conversation was going.

'That leaves one, eh, girl,' said Helen, stumbling over the word as she anxiously avoided using the word 'whore'. Embarrassment was also deeply etched in red all over her face. But she continued anyway. 'I believe one of the girls is called Sadie. If you want to put her in the room next to me, I'll be happy to keep an eye on her for you,' said Helen.

So it was arranged. Helen moved into the saloon and much to Colorado's dismay, Sadie occupied the room next to her. Whilst he had nothing to hide, the prospect of the two women conversing with one another, perhaps even discussing their respective relationships with him, was most embarrassing.

There was nothing Colorado could do about it, however. So instead, he enjoyed a well-earned beer in the bar. His thoughts turned towards the buffalo hunters' chief scout. Remembering Trooper Smith's warning, he was ready for anything. The man might be a bounty hunter or perhaps a gunslinger looking to make a reputation for himself. Less likely, yet not impossible, the man might be a Ranger. Colorado was aware that the Rangers, disbanded after the end of the Civil War by the Yankees because of their well-known support for the Confederacy, had been recently reconstituted and were now called the Texas Rangers. Yet, as he entered the saloon, the buffalo hunters' chief scout proved to be none of these.

Dressed in a buckskin jacket, tough and wiry as Panhandle grass, he was about six feet tall. His craggy, weather-beaten face gave little indication of his age; his long golden brown hair, plaited at the back, was still too long to remain hidden under his beige-coloured Stetson which sported a single black feather. He also had a distinctive goatee beard in which a few white hairs had begun to mingle with the golden brown. His very expensive riding boots were made of kidskin, not leather and around his waist was a massive gun-belt. From it, on his right hip, hung an equally massive — if ancient — Dragoon Colt six-gun, carried in a cut-away holster. From the other hip hung an equally impressive-looking Bowie knife. He looked the archetypical Indian fighter, which indeed he had once been. Colorado recognized him instantly and his face broke out into a broad smile.

'With most of the Apaches tamed, hunting buffalo, what else would a man with my name be doing?' laughed the scout. 'I've also been looking for you but I'm afraid I may not be the only one.'

His problems with Helen temporarily forgotten, over a beer or three, the old friends swapped yarns. Then Buffalo related his meeting with Maine and the reason the lawyer had paid him so much to search for Colorado.

'But I don't trust Maine. It may be only a coincidence, but almost as soon as I left him, I got the strongest feeling I was being shadowed.'

9

Trooper Smith brought Helen's luggage to her new bedroom, which looked like a harlot's boudoir and smelt of cheap perfume — the same perfume that had clung to Colorado after he had returned from his trip to Adobe Wells.

Helen knew she had no claim on Colorado. Indeed, he had said from the outset that he would be moving on. Then there was this dance hall girl called Sadie. Had this been her room? Had Sadie and Colorado made love in the bed in which she was now expected to sleep? Of course, she couldn't be jealous of a saloon girl who sold her body for a living. Or could she? She tried to dismiss the idea as ridiculous but failed abysmally.

A rather timid knock on her bedroom door interrupted the flow of her thoughts. She looked at the huge bed and blushed as she thought, no hoped, it might be

Colorado. But instead, it was a young woman. From her daringly low-cut dress, bare shoulders and overdone make-up, Helen correctly guessed her visitor was a saloon girl.

'I'm Sadie,' she said. 'The lieutenant said you had arranged for me to have the next room. I wanted to thank you and also ask you why?'

'It seems we know the same man,' replied Helen curtly. 'Come in and close the door.'

Sadie entered and sat down. Helen began to question her. Nervously, at first, Sadie began to speak about her life as a saloon girl. As she did so, Helen studied her closely. She had formed a fixed picture of what saloon girls, especially Sadie, looked like. Yet, in spite of her overdone make-up and risqué dress, the young girl sitting demurely (as anyone could in such a low-cut dress) did not comply with that picture. She was much younger and Helen could visualize a girl who might be quite pretty.

That should have made Helen feel even more jealous. Yet it did not. As they talked and she learnt more about the unfortunate circumstances leading to Sadie becoming a saloon girl, Helen's opinion began to change. Indeed, as hard as she tried, she could not dislike her rival. Quite the contrary, and that gave her an idea …

Next morning, the lieutenant called a meeting in his hastily converted office. After a few minutes, Colorado and Buffalo arrived, followed by a tired-looking Trooper Smith; he had been scouting all night.

'Sit down, gentlemen,' said the lieutenant. 'Before we begin, apart from Miss Blaine, who will be joining us shortly, there may be another lady within hearing distance, so keep your voices down. I don't want her overhearing bits of conversation which, if repeated around Adobe Wells, might cause undue alarm.'

'Quite right. Panic-stricken settlers are the last thing we need,' said Buffalo.

'Anything to report, Trooper?' asked the lieutenant.

'Nothing, sir. Nary a sign of the Indians.'

'Thank you, Trooper. You are dismissed. Grab a bite to eat and then get some rest. You may be needed again tonight,' said the lieutenant.

The lieutenant waited until Trooper Smith had left and then continued.

'Gentlemen, my orders are to deny the hostiles use of this settlement and I will carry those out in full. I do not intend to seek out the hostiles but when necessary we will fight, whatever the consequences.'

There was a knock at the door and Helen entered. In spite of his lowered voice, the ashen look on her face indicated she had overheard the lieutenant.

'Gentlemen, I've asked Miss Blaine to attend because she has had many dealings with Quanah Parker and can hopefully shed some light on what the hostiles might do next. Please sit down, Miss Blaine.'

'Hostiles?' asked Helen.

122

'It's what the Army calls the Indian tribes who didn't sign the Treaty of '67,' said Buffalo as he introduced himself. 'Pardon me if my words offend or cause alarm, Miss Blaine, but I'm a blunt man and our situation demands straight talking.'

'Don't mind me, Mr Buffalo,' she replied. 'We Texas girls prefer straight talking.'

'Then let me start,' said Colorado. 'Counting both war parties we met coming here, plus Quanah's band, I make it at least seventy braves, all armed with repeating rifles or shotguns.'

'Why do you think they did not attack the wagon train?' asked the lieutenant.

Helen explained about the immunity Quanah's pennant had given the little wagon train.

'Miss Blaine, do you think the pennant will provide immunity for Adobe Wells?' asked the lieutenant.

'No. Some time ago, Quanah told me that their medicine man, Isa-Tai, claimed to have had two visions. The first, to have been chosen by the Great Spirit to unite all Indians who oppose the Peace Treaty, whatever their tribe, and then lead them to victory. I believe Adobe Wells is to be the test of Isa-Tai's vision.'

'And his second so-called vision?' asked Buffalo sceptically.

'Quanah told me that Isa-Tai claimed that in a revelation, he has been shown how to make a special black war paint which will protect the Indians against the white man's bullets.'

'Miss Blaine, do you think Quanah believes that?' asked the lieutenant.

'No. He believes that Isa-Tai's claim is superstitious nonsense. Nevertheless I understand that the medicine man has a strong following. Indians from other tribes have already begun to flock to his cause. For that reason, Quanah wears black war paint and follows Isa-Tai even though he told me he doesn't really believe in him.'

They were interrupted by a knock on the door. It was Sadie bringing coffee for all. But it was a Sadie like no man had ever seen her. She was wearing a delightfully demure pink dress borrowed from Helen. Her newly washed hair was swept back and neatly tied. Indeed, apart from the twinkle in her eyes, all traces of the saloon girl she had once been had been eradicated. To Colorado, the swiftness and the effect of the transition were amazing. Indeed, he hardly recognized her.

If Colorado was more than a little taken aback, then Buffalo was rendered speechless. He looked at Sadie as if he had never seen her before. Helen was delighted with her protégée's new look and the effect it had on the men, especially Buffalo. As there was little more she could add to the meeting, she left with Sadie.

'Now that the ladies have gone, we have to decide what's best to do,' said the lieutenant. 'From what Miss Blaine has just told us, the hostiles will attack us. So before they do, I would like to get the women and children out of Adobe Wells.'

'No. Wagons, especially the ox-drawn ones, are too slow,' countered Buffalo.

'Buffalo is right,' agreed Colorado. 'Even if the wagons had a good start — and that's not likely if Quanah sends out scouts — the Indians would easily catch up with them. Then, they would slaughter the men and take the children back to their lodges to be brought up as Comanche. As for the women, the lucky ones would be the ones killed during the raid.'

'Possibly, Colorado, but I was thinking of sending you, Buffalo and his hunters to protect the wagon train,' said the lieutenant.

'Splitting our forces would be a disaster,' Buffalo replied. 'Without the buffalo hunters, how long can your troops hold out? Most likely the Indians will attack at dawn. Even if you're not overrun in their first assault, you will be dead by sunset.'

'I fail to see how a handful of buffalo hunters will make that much difference,' replied the lieutenant coldly.

'Trust me, with their fire power we

have a chance but only if we fortify the buildings and build a barricade in front of the stable,' replied Buffalo.

'Why build a barricade?'

'There are rooms above the stable. Provided the stables aren't set alight by the Indians, the rooms are by far the safest in the settlement. We should put the women and children in them.'

'There's plenty of timber in the stable yard, or at least there was when I was here a few weeks ago,' said Colorado.

'I'd rather use it to fortify the other buildings,' said Buffalo.

'Very well, no wagon train,' said the lieutenant. 'Buffalo, you may have my written authority to requisition everything you need.'

'I'll need men, too,' said Buffalo.

'Colorado, round up all the male settlers and civilians and bring them to the saloon. Take Trooper Smith and a couple of other troopers. You may need to persuade some of them to come with you,' ordered the lieutenant.

'Promise the men a couple of free

drinks and you won't need any troops to persuade them,' said Buffalo cynically.

He was right. Colorado had no difficulty in rounding up all the male settlers. After the promised drinks, the lieutenant explained the dangers of trying to get a wagon train away from Adobe Wells. For someone who had previously been in favour of sending out a wagon train, he painted a dreadfully graphic picture of the likely outcome of such an action — so graphic that even the few settlers who possessed their own horses voted to stay.

Buffalo then explained what had to be done to fortify the buildings and the settlers set about it with a will. And there was a bonus: two of them were skilled carpenters. They had been on their way to Arizona to start up a business in Lincoln County before being caught up in the Indian rising. The lieutenant put them in charge of the alterations.

All the downstairs windows of the three main buildings were given new, heavy-duty shutters. Next, the swing doors of the saloon were removed and the entrance boarded up, leaving only a small and easily defendable door at the rear of the saloon.

The troopers took no part in the reconstruction but stood guard duty at night.

So, even with the considerable help of the buffalo hunters, it still took two days to complete the work. Even then, Buffalo was not satisfied. Fire was a real threat to all the buildings in Adobe Wells so after further consultation with the lieutenant, he ordered the belongings and goods to be removed from three of the settlers' wagons and then refilled them with every empty barrel that could be found.

Under heavy escort, the wagons were driven to the South Canadian river where the empty containers were filled.

On return, half of the barrels were shared between the main buildings to provide water for their occupants in the event of a siege and the remainder were similarly divided and then laboriously lifted on to the flat roofs of the buildings.

In the event of fire arrows, their water could then be used to douse any fires.

The rest of the settlers' wagons, emptied of the goods they had been carrying, were then driven across the front of the stable yard. Next, their horses or oxen were unharnessed; the horses were led to the new corral and the oxen were allowed to make their own way to the open range to graze on whatever grass they could find. As for water, the beasts were quite capable of finding their way to the South Canadian River without any guidance from their owners.

The wagons were tipped over on to their sides thus forming a substantial barricade behind which the male settlers could fight. However, a narrow pathway was left to provide access to, or escape from, the livery stable in the event of an emergency.

While the men worked on the defences, their wives cooked and continuously served meals in the mess tent. Colorado thought they had the rough end of the deal, but was wise enough to keep his thoughts to himself.

It took an anxious four days to complete all the work, during which time there was no sign of the Kwahadi or any other Indian tribe. Then, to minimize the danger of a surprise attack, Colorado and Buffalo began scouting missions. However, unknown to them, their missions were unnecessary. Many miles away, Isa-Tai was gathering bands of rebellious Indians together. To unite them under his leadership, he led them in a Sun Dance. It was the first time in their long history that the Comanche had involved themselves in such a ritual.

Quanah Parker was also present although he did not take part in the ritualized Sun Dance. He did not believe in the supposed powers of the Sun Dance or Isa-Tai. Yet for his own ambitious reasons, he had pledged his support to the medicine man. Why? Well Isa-Tai was no warrior. Therefore, he would need someone to lead his braves when they attacked Adobe Wells. Quanah intended to be that leader. If the raid succeeded he would gain great kudos. On the other hand, should the attack fail, Isa-Tai would then shoulder all the blame.

Back at Adobe Wells, continuous daily scouting had given Colorado little time to talk to Helen. In any case, apart from Petra, Sadie seemed to be her constant companion and he did not relish meeting his former mistresses together. Buffalo, of course, had no such problem and spent all the time that could be spared from scouting in their company. However, much to Colorado's relief, it was evident that the object of the scout's romantic interest was Sadie and not Helen.

10

With a rifle-like sound, the main post of the buffalo hunters' tent suddenly cracked. Buffalo just managed to scramble outside before the tent collapsed. In the eerie, pre-dawn half-light he could just make out a number of Kwahadi braves creeping towards the main buildings. Unusually, they were attacking on foot.

Swiftly, he drew his old Dragoon Colt and fired three shots into the air, the warning signal an Indian attack was imminent. The element of surprise lost, the Kwahadi hesitated. During that moment, troopers poured out of their tents and although only half-dressed, opened fire. However, still half-asleep, their shooting was ragged. Although some of the Indians were hit, most were able to retreat uninjured. Once out of rifle range they stopped and waited for new orders. However, his plan thwarted, Isa-Tai hesitated.

Roused by the gunfire, the civilian settlers awoke and scurried out of their tents — some carrying, some dragging their children as they dashed for the safety of the stable yard. They entered it in single file down the narrow passageway between the upturned wagons; it had been left open for an emergency such as this. A queue soon formed, leaving the settlers extremely vulnerable had the Indians attacked. Fortunately for the settlers, the Kwahadi were unaware of the situation so again failed to press home their advantage. Then, as the last settler passed through the passageway, it was blocked by a couple of troopers using timber left for just such a purpose. They remained behind the barricades to take charge of the settlers.

Once inside the stable yard the female settlers and their children discovered the entrance to the actual stables had been boarded up. The two troopers then directed the women and children to a ladder which led up to the relative safety of the stable's upper floor.

One by one, they climbed up the ladder. The children managed easily. The women, conscious of losing their modesty even though most of them were wearing ground-length skirts, found the ladder climb more difficult to negotiate. Much to their surprise, they were met at the top by Ami, still dressed in her racy saloon clothes. Betsy, the other saloon girl, had been one of the very few people who had decided to leave Adobe Wells. Ami guided them to their pre-designated emergency quarters. These were nothing more than sheets of canvas draped from the ceiling to the floor forming temporary cubicles, but at least they gave the families a semblance of privacy. However, the male settlers deemed old enough to fight remained in the yard below and took up positions behind the overturned wagons.

Meanwhile, the buffalo hunters, carrying their formidable Sharps rifles, headed for the second-floor rooms of the hardware store. Buffalo did not join them; instead, he headed for the saloon. Of course, he had to use the back door as the swing doors at the front had been boarded up.

Sadie, Helen and Petra were locked inside Helen's bedroom above the saloon. This was for their safety. Nevertheless, Petra complained bitterly that after the training she had received from Colorado, she should be fighting with the settlers. However, Helen angrily refused to let her join them. So, to keep the peace, Colorado found Petra a spare carbine and a box of ammunition and told her to use it to defend Helen and Sadie in the event of any Kwahadi forcing their way into the saloon. Only slightly mollified, Petra took up position by the window instead.

Isa-Tai continued to hesitate. Then, instead of attacking, he sought inspiration from yet another Sun Dance. Not until the long ritual was finished was he prepared to order the next raid. Consequently, all was ready in Adobe Wells when the Kwahadi actually attacked.

This time, on horseback and led by Quanah Parker, the Kwahadi-Comanche charged. They were not alone. Supporting them were members of other sub-tribes of the Comanche, untamed Kiowa braves who had migrated from east Texas rather than live in reservations, renegade Cheyennes and from the northern prairies, even some Mandan warriors. Yet, well before they were in range of the settlement's carbines, they ran into a fearsome barrage of bullets which came, not from the troopers, but from the Sharp rifles of the buffalo hunters stationed above the hardware store. In spite of the extreme range, several Indians fell from their mustangs.

From the lieutenant's office, Buffalo also opened fire. Even though the charging Indians were still well out of range of ordinary carbines, his buffalo-rifle found its target. As Quanah had feared, the so-called magical properties of Isa-Tai's black warrior war paint proved useless.

As the charging Indians neared the buildings, the troopers opened fire; the Indians' black paint proved to be equally useless against their weapons. Then, from the lieutenant's office, Colorado and the lieutenant joined in. Yet although they suffered heavy losses, the Indians continued their headlong gallop towards Adobe Wells.

From behind the barricade of upturned wagons came yet another volley. This time it was from the male settlers. It was the last straw. As this unexpected barrage reigned down upon them, the Indians turned and retreated back to their lines.

Isa-Tai broke out into a chant which lasted several minutes. Then, with the promise their black war paint would this time protect them from the palefaces' bullets; he gave the signal for Quanah and his war party to charge again.

Lying almost flat on their mustangs, the war party raced back to Adobe Wells. But, at the same range as before, they were met by a devastating barrage of fire from the deadly Sharps rifles of the buffalo hunters.

But this time, Quanah did not lead his war party directly towards the settlement. Instead, he ordered the war party to start a series of zigzag manoeuvres hoping to make them harder to hit. To no avail; they suffered even more casualties before they reached the upturned wagons. Then, still led by Quanah, those braves still able to dismounted and began to attack on foot.

Neither the troopers in the stable loft nor the buffalo hunters in the hardware store could fire at the Indians for fear of hitting the settlers. In spite of their losses, the rampaging Indians still heavily outnumbered them. It seemed inevitable: the barricade must be overrun.

But one man had foreseen the danger: Trooper Smith. From seemingly out of nowhere, he led a counter attack. Quanah was forced to dispatch a small party of his braves to quell the danger. Then, with the remainder of his braves, he resumed his attack on the barricade.

Trooper Smith put back the years to when he had a command in the Confederate Army. He issued an order.

Instantly, his troopers reached down to their scabbards. However, these troopers had served in the Confederacy during the Civil War. So their scabbards contained shotguns not sabres as used by most of the rest of the cavalry.

Too late, Quanah saw the danger. There was nothing he could do to prevent his braves racing headlong into the deadly shotgun barrage. Mortified, the Kwahadi sub-chief could only watch as his braves were literally ripped to shreds. It was too much for him to bear, so he called off the attack and again retreated.

Isa-Tai then turned to his reserves: Arapaho, Kiowa and Cheyenne braves who, dismayed by the Peace Treaty with the paleskins, had joined his cause. Urged on by the medicine man, they joined up with Quanah's braves. The Indians attacked yet again.

Possessed by an overwhelming desire to atone for the death of his braves, Quanah pressed forward, regardless of his own safety. This time, he reached the front of the saloon. But as its entrance had been boarded up, no matter how hard he tried, he could not force an entrance and beat his fists on the boards in sheer frustration.

However, bullets thudding into the wall beside him brought the Kwahadi chief back to his senses. He remounted his mustang and again signalled a retreat to the position held by Isa-Tai.

In spite of the heavy losses, Isa-Tai was still confident of victory. At his command the combined tribes of Indians mounted yet another attack. Yet again they were repulsed, again with heavy losses.

But problems were mounting up for the defenders. The settlers behind the overturned wagons were out of ammunition, so led by the two troopers delegated to lead them, they were forced to retreat and climb up to the stable loft.

Lack of ammunition for the remarkable Sharps rifle was also beginning to become a problem for the buffalo hunters. In fact, they had originally come to Adobe Wells to await the arrival of provisions and ammunition in a wagon train. Of course, the nature of the wagon train's cargo meant it had to be escorted by the cavalry. But, so far neither the cavalry nor the wagon train had arrived. Nor was either expected in the immediate future.

A little over two years prior, after an outstanding career, Colonel McKenzie had been given command of the 4th Cavalry with specific instructions to end the raiding of the Comanche and force them on to a reservation set aside for them in the Indian Territories.

However, although things had not always gone in the favour of the Kwahadi, the 4th Cavalry had come out second best during that campaign and McKenzie had been wounded. An arrow in his thigh had forced him and the 4th to temporarily withdraw. But McKenzie learnt from these setbacks; sabres had been discarded and replaced by shotguns. Crow Indians, traditional enemies of the Comanche, had been recruited to scout for the 4th and train its troopers in the art of Indian fighting.

In spite of the messenger sent by the lieutenant, it had been this special training that had delayed the wagon train. Somehow the settlement had to hold out until it arrived. How this was to be achieved, the lieutenant had no idea. Fortunately there was someone who did.

Without a word, Buffalo adjusted the telescopic sights of his Sharps rifle and moved to the window. Colorado had never before encountered telescopic sights, so had little idea of the advantage they gave.

'What are you going to do, shoot jack rabbits?' he mocked.

'Look and learn, my friend,' Buffalo said and then called to the lieutenant to join them.

Thinking he was well out of range, Isa-Tai had taken up position on a knoll about fifteen hundred yards from the saloon. With him was a select band of Kwahadi braves, including Quanah.

Buffalo took careful aim and then fired. Amazingly, three quarters of a mile away on the knoll, a brave fell as if he had been pole-axed. A second shot rang out and Quanah fell to the ground although he was not dead. The bullet had ricocheted off a nearby rock, grazing his temple and temporarily stunning him.

Even so, the effect on the Kwahadi was devastating. Not only had the supposedly magical war paint of Isa-Tai failed to ward off the paleskins' bullets, but in their eyes their hated enemy had a new magic which could strike them from afar.

Word spread rapidly among the braves from the other Indian tribes. They too were devastated. Although Quanah recovered, it was too late; all Isa-Tai's reinforcements withdrew.

Not that Quanah did anything to quell their withdrawal. Isa-Tai had been utterly discredited by their defeat. There would be need for a new leader and Quanah intended to become that leader. Only then could he avenge the humiliating defeat the Kwahadi had suffered — humiliating because only a total of twenty-eight troopers, buffalo hunters and settlers had withstood overwhelming odds to defy the might of the Kwahadi.

It was probably two shots from the

Sharps rifle that actually saved the day. Nevertheless, Buffalo despised the weapon. Over a well-earned beer that night, he explained why.

'Once, I had to track buffalos for days and then use all my stalking skills to get close enough to kill one. Now, with my Sharps rifle I can stop even the largest bull at six hundred yards,' he said bitterly.

'Isn't that good, my old friend?' asked Colorado.

'No. Do you know how many buffalo I killed before I found you?'

'No,' replied Colorado.

'Two hundred. Back east they've discovered a way of tanning buffalo hides to make them commercially viable, so each hide is worth three dollars,' replied Buffalo.

'Six hundred dollars in a month? You're almost rich!' exclaimed Colorado.

'Not in a month. I shot two hundred buffalo in each and every day for a month. In the end I had fifteen skinners working full time for me.'

'Six hundred dollars a day! Even after

paying the skinners and transport costs, you must be very rich. So what's the problem?' asked the lieutenant.

'The other buffalo hunters. Maybe they weren't all as good a shot as me, but even so, there's hardly any buffalos left east of Adobe Wells. That's why hunters intend to go west into the Staked Plains. I tried to dissuade them but they wouldn't listen, there's too much money at stake. What do they care that the Kwahadi and the rest of the hostile Indians won't tolerate them hunting in what they consider to be their hunting grounds? They expect to be fully protected by the cavalry.'

'But there aren't enough troopers al-located to Texas to protect the Mexican border, patrol the rest of the Panhandle and baby-sit the buffalo hunters. So what do you think the Kwahadi will do?' asked the lieutenant.

'Surely that will depend on where the cavalry are deployed,' said Colorado.

'Well, politics as much as the Apache will mean that no troops will be moved away from the Rio Grande. Not that I think that the Mexican Army will ever again cross the border,' said Buffalo.

'Although I have orders from Colonel McKenzie to hold Adobe Wells, I also have orders, countersigned by the President, to render the buffalo hunters every assistance. So, until they are countermanded, here I stay,' said the lieutenant ruefully.

'Then I guess the Kwahadi will regroup and then go on the rampage. No settlement or ranch in the western Panhandle will be safe,' said Buffalo grimly.

In spite of any doubts he may have had, the lieutenant got on with his duties. A check on casualties revealed three dead and eight wounded. Fortunately, none of the wounded were seriously hurt.

It was impossible to calculate how many Indians had been slain because, during their retreats, they had tried to take their dead back with them. Nevertheless, thirteen of their number lay dead. More to avoid giving distress to the women and children than for any other reason, the lieutenant ordered their burial. Trooper Smith was put in charge of the troops instructed to carry out this unpleasant chore.

Next day, Buffalo, Colorado and Trooper Smith scouted the area. All the signs indicated the Kwahadi had left and done so in great haste. Buffalo correctly guessed they had gone away to select a new leader. The abject failure of the Adobe Wells raid had engendered much anger amongst the Indians and Isa-Tai was the focus of that anger. They had flocked to his summons because the medicine man had claimed his magical black war paint would protect them against the paleskins' bullets. Of course, it had not done so.

By wearing the so-called magical war paint, it seemed to the rest of the Indians, especially the Kwahadi, that Quanah had been duped just as they had. So Isa-Tai and not Quanah was blamed for the failure. As a result, Isa-Tai's previously unchallenged influence over the various Comanche sub-tribes was shattered beyond redemption and he faded into oblivion.

Buffalo had correctly prophesied that the Kwahadi would regroup but he believed it would be under the leadership of Bull Bear, the overall chief of all of the Kwahadi. Of course, he had no way of knowing that at that moment Bull Bear lay desperately ill, suffering from pneumonia.

He did not recover. After the Chief's death, Quanah achieved his ambition and became the undisputed leader of not only the Kwahadi but of all the Indians in the north west of Texas and the Indian Territories who opposed the Peace Treaty with Washington. However, the process of Quanah's inauguration was a lengthy one and that gave the inhabitants of Adobe Wells the time they needed to regroup.

11

Some weeks after the attack had been repelled, a cavalry rider arrived bearing dispatches for the lieutenant. They came from Colonel McKenzie; the 4th Cavalry had been temporarily re-assigned. They had been ordered to escort once-hostile Indians to their reservation situated several weeks of hard riding from Adobe Wells. As a result, the wagon train which should have been carrying ammunition for the buffalo hunters and supplies to the settlement had been cancelled.

Once they heard the news, the buffalo hunters held a meeting. They decided to abandon hunting for the rest of the year and to return to the safety of their headquarters in Kansas. Once they left, the Kwahadi had no reason to attack the settlement. Instead, as Buffalo had predicted, once Quanah had been appointed their leader, the Kwahadi began to exact their revenge — not against the settlement at Adobe Wells but southwards across the western Texas Panhandle, only ending when they almost reached traditional Apache territory near the Mexican border.

Quanah had learnt from the mistakes made at Adobe Wells; no isolated settlement or even large ranches in the path of the Kwahadi rampage were able to withstand the Indians, who took neither prisoners nor hostages. Instead, they butchered everyone they captured.

As the news of the Kwahadi's new strategy filtered through to Adobe Wells, the lieutenant, acting under fresh orders, began the evacuation of the little settlement. Helen decided to return to her homestead, although she expected Colorado to remain in Adobe Wells with Ami or even Sadie.

In the saloon that night, over a couple of warm beers, Buffalo again recounted his reasons for coming to Adobe Wells.

'I'd been following your trail for weeks

when I fell in with the buffalo hunters. Used the money Maine paid me to find you to buy a Sharps rifle.'

'I'm glad you did. In your hands it's a hell of a weapon. I've never seen anything like those telescopic sights,' said Colorado. 'But why did Maine pay you to find me?'

'Seems you've come into a mighty big inheritance. A sack full of money and a large plantation complete with a mansion-sized house, and its own sawmill which also had its own house. Said he'd been hired by its executors to find you. So what are you going to do?'

'Damned if I know. I was heading for Lincoln County in New Mexico. A couple of ranches are hiring top guns for good money. I was on my way there when I stupidly got myself bushwhacked. Helen helped me recover. I was paying her back by helping out on her ranch when the Indian rising erupted.'

'She's a remarkable woman. A man could do a lot worse.'

'She deserves a lot better than a

professional gunfighter with a price on his head,' replied Colorado bitterly.

'A man can change, especially when he's come into a powerful lot of land and money. You could start a new life.'

'But what do I know about running a plantation?'

'There's bound to be a manager already running it. In any case, you could learn. There was a time when you didn't know how to handle a six-gun and I had to teach you. Look at you now. Apart from Cobb, I guess you must be about the fastest gun in Texas.'

'Sometimes, old friend, I wish I'd never learnt,' said Colorado ruefully. 'But what are you going to do?'

'Until they join up with Colonel McKenzie and the Fourth Cavalry, the lieutenant wants me to scout for his troopers. After that, who knows?'

'What about Sadie? I've seen the way you've been looking at her. With the money you've earned, she could sure do worse and you're not getting any younger; it's time you settled down.'

'She's sure scrubbed up real pretty. But even though she was a saloon girl, looking is all I've been doing,' said Buffalo hastily. 'I wasn't sure whether she or Helen was your girl.'

'Anything between Sadie and me is over and done with. It was always going to be that way. As for Helen, like I say, I had intended to move on. Now, I'm not sure what I'm going to do.'

For a brief moment the idea of sharing his new inheritance with Helen and Petra flitted across his mind, but he was still a wanted man with a bounty on his head. There would always be another young gunslinger looking to make a name for himself by collecting that bounty. Sooner or later, especially as he got older, it was inevitable one of them would prove to be the faster. Unless, of course, some posse caught up with him first. So he dismissed the idea of settling down and changed the subject.

'Buffalo, what made you decide to give up being a sheriff and ride hundreds of miles to find me?' he asked instead.

'Boredom; the town was dead. That and the money Maine gave me to find you. But I'm not the only one looking for you; I believe Cobb may be after you. At first, I didn't realize he was trailing me. Luckily, he's a gunman not a scout so I eventually spotted him. Unfortunately, by then, the damage was done.'

'How did you know it was Cobb?'

'Remember Jed Blake?'

'Sure, until he met his match, folks used to claim his draw was faster than lightning.'

'I was with Blake in Waynoka when Cobb rode into town. Cool as you like, he challenged Blake to a showdown the next day.'

'Why the next day?' asked Colorado.

'Cobb said he wanted a big crowd for the gunfight. Then, whatever the outcome, they could tell everyone they had seen the fastest gun in Texas.'

'What happened?'

'Cobb outdrew Blake, fair and square. Shot him between the eyes before Blake's guns cleared leather. Bragged about it afterwards. Reckoned he always drilled his opponent between the eyes, just to please the crowd.'

'So what did you do when you realized Cobb was tailing you?' asked Colorado.

'I wasn't about to tangle with a gunman as fast as Cobb. Nor was I going to lead him to you. That's why I bought the buffalo rifle and joined the hunters.'

'What did Cobb do then?' asked Colorado.

'Hung around for some time and then he moved on. I guess so many skinners working for me convinced him that I had stopped looking for you.'

'But how did he know you were looking for me?' asked Colorado.

'Somebody in California stands to inherit the spread if you don't. So what if he paid the man hired by the executors to find you and then make sure that you didn't live long enough to inherit the plantation?'

'You mean Maine hired Cobb as well as you?'

'Can you think of a better way to get

rid of the man they call Colorado?'

'You've seen Cobb draw. Do you reckon he's faster than me?'

'Yes. He's a natural born killer, you ain't. I reckon that gives him the edge.'

'What if I leave Texas? Do you think he will still come after me?'

'No doubt about it,' replied Buffalo.

'In his warped mind he would believe that people would say that he was only the fastest draw in Texas as long as you stayed out of the Lone Star State. But I doubt if he knows your real name. Why have you kept it secret all these years?'

'At first, I didn't want my people to know where I was and then, when I began to get into trouble, I didn't want them to be embarrassed by my actions.'

'Understandable, I guess. But there are many Texans like me who think that the charges against you were railroaded through the courts because you dared to side with the sodbusters against the Yankee carpetbaggers.'

'Doesn't make any difference. As long as I got such a big price on my head,

157

bounty hunters are bound to come after me,' said Colorado bitterly.

'Then why not go back to Richmond. Leave your old life and name behind you and make a fresh start.'

'When I show up to claim my inheritance, what's to stop Maine sending for Cobb or hiring some other gunfighter ?'

'You got me there,' admitted Buffalo. 'But leave it to me. I got you into this mess, so it's up to me to get you out of it.'

'Fine, but no violence. We have no real evidence that Maine hired Cobb. As unlikely as it seems, it may just be a coincidence.'

'OK. If that's the way you want it, you have my word, I won't kill him.'

However, a germ of an idea came into Buffalo's mind, even as he spoke. There might be a way to put an end to Maine without breaking his word to Colorado.

12

Early next morning, Helen, with Petra at her side, set out for her ranch. Much to her surprise, they were accompanied by Colorado. In fact, the lieutenant — unable to provide an escort because of his depleted force — had insisted he did so. Not that Colorado had needed much persuasion.

They had an uneventful journey back to Helen's little ranch. The weather was hot and the dusty trail deserted. As soon as they arrived, Colorado and Petra unloaded the meagre supply of provisions Helen had been able to get from Adobe Wells. It didn't take long, so they had time to tend to the horses and wash off the trail dust before Helen finished cooking the evening meal.

After dinner was over, and Petra had gone to bed, Colorado suggested she should leave her ranch until the Indian unrest had died down.

'There's no telling which other tribes might join up with the Kwahadi and they might not all honour Quanah's pledge not to attack you,' he said.

'The lieutenant said the same. But tell me, where would I go and how would I live?' replied Helen.

'I hadn't thought that far ahead,' admitted Colorado.

'Well, until you come up with a better plan, I stay here with Petra,' she said defiantly.

Was that a hint? Was Helen implying she would come with him if he asked her? Colorado dismissed the idea instantly. With Cobb on his trail, the only life he could offer her was even more dangerous than staying on her ranch. And then there was young Petra. Surely she deserved someone better than an outlaw and a gunslinger to act as a father figure.

Although Helen insisted Colorado slept in the ranch house and not the barn, there was no further romance between them. Helen remained friendly, but somehow, she had managed to construct an invisible barrier through which Colorado could not penetrate.

He tried to convince himself that it was for the best. He didn't want her around when he met Cobb as he knew he must. Buffalo had said Cobb was the faster on the draw. But was death at the hands of Cobb as inevitable as it seemed?

As the days went slowly by, Colorado started to teach Petra again and once again the youngster applied herself diligently. However, she also began to ask a number of awkward questions.

'Aunt Helen said you will be leaving us soon. Don't you like us anymore?'

'Of course I do. It's just best for everybody that I leave.'

'Why?' Petra asked with child-like directness.

'Because of some things I did a long time ago I have to leave and live far away,' replied Colorado, choosing his words carefully.

'Then take Aunt Helen and me with you.'

'Too dangerous. We don't want your aunt to get hurt, do we?'

'But Quanah won't hurt us if we all go away together,' protested Petra.

'Perhaps not. But there is another man who is after me and he might.'

'Then, let me help; teach me how to shoot a six-gun like you.'

'No, not like me, Petra. But I will teach you how to shoot straight.'

'If you are still determined to leave us, it might be a good idea if you taught us both how to shoot a six-gun,' interrupted Helen.

Colorado had been so preoccupied answering Petra's questions, he hadn't noticed Helen. She had been standing behind him long enough to overhear what he had been saying.

'Very well, if that's what you want,' he replied.

That evening, in Adobe Wells, Sadie was thinking hard about her future. She had moved into the room temporarily occupied by Helen but as yet, she had no desire to return to her former profession. However, her money had almost run out and she knew that to survive, she must soon do so.

But not tonight. In spite of his back-woodsman appearance and forthright manner, she liked Buffalo very much. She had a special evening planned in which dinner in her room was only to be the starter. Nevertheless, she didn't doubt it was only her body he wanted. After which, like so many before him, he would be on his way, never to return.

During dinner, Buffalo was unusually quiet. It seemed to Sadie that he was summoning up courage to ask her something and she had a pretty good idea what it was he wanted.

'Sadie,' he said at last, 'seeing as you've changed your ways somewhat, I guess you must be running short of money.'

She thought she knew what was coming and nodded her head in agreement.

'Well, I have to leave in the morning. The lieutenant and his men are pulling out and the lieutenant wants me to scout for them. They've had orders to join up with the 4th Cavalry near Clayton, a town where I used to be the sheriff. When the lieutenant and his men have rejoined the 4th, their leader, Colonel McKenzie, is going after Kwahadi-Comanche again.'

During his scouting missions Buffalo had unearthed evidence to suggest that there were war parties other than Kwahadi involved in the raids. However, whether they were working with or separately to Quanah, he had not yet found out, so he kept that part of his news from Sadie.

'And you are going with them, I suppose,' said Sadie sadly.

'I'm only scouting for the lieutenant's troopers until they join up with the 4th Cavalry. Apparently Colonel McKenzie's got himself some Crow Indian scouts, so my services won't be required after that.'

'Will you go back to buffalo hunting?' asked Sadie.

'No, I have to put right a mistake I've made. Me and my big mouth have gotten my best friend into real trouble.'

'Colorado?' asked Sadie.

Without going into details of Colorado's inheritance, Buffalo explained his encounter with Maine and his belief the lawyer had then hired the best gunfighter money could buy to follow him until he found Colorado.

'I can't do anything about Cobb. I'm pretty good with a six-gun but I'm not in his class, but then nobody is,' Buffalo said bitterly.

'Not even Colorado?' asked Sadie.

'I doubt it. But even if he is, Maine will just go on hiring more gunmen until one finally outdraws or bushwhacks Colorado. So I have to stop Maine.'

'But if you've promised Colorado you won't kill the man, how can you do that?' asked Sadie.

'More than one way to skin a buffalo,' said the scout mysteriously. 'But talking of buffalos reminds me. Here's a little of the money I made from hunting them. Should be enough to keep you going until I get back.'

Buffalo dug into the pocket of his deerskin jacket and gave Sadie a stack of dollars. It was a very generous amount, many times more than she usually received for her *special* services. Slowly, in order to tease him a little, she began to unbutton the front of her dress. To her amazement, he stopped her.

'I guess you've known a few men who made promises, all vowing they would come back, and I bet not many of them did,' said Buffalo gently.

'None,' admitted Sadie.

'And they all swore that this time it would be different.'

Sadie nodded her head in agreement. She could not trust herself to speak.

'Well, if my plan backfires, I may not come back either,' said Buffalo. 'But if I can outsmart a smart aleck lawyer, I'll come back for you and claim what's mine.'

'You don't have to pay me for that, I'll go to bed with you for free,' she said, pushing the pile of money towards him.

'Hell, that ain't what that's for,' he said gruffly as he pushed the pile of money back to her. 'In any case, one time with

166

you ain't near enough.'

He kissed her lightly on her cheek and, leaving the money on the table, was gone before she could ask him what he meant by his last remark.

Would he come back for her? In spite of many promises she had received to the contrary, no man had ever done so. So why should Buffalo be any different? Yet he hadn't touched her and he'd left enough money to keep her going for many weeks. Well then, she would wait for him until the money ran out. After that? She simply didn't know.

13

Well before Sadie awoke, the lieutenant, the troopers and Buffalo rode out of Adobe Wells. They were headed eastwards to rendezvous with Colonel McKenzie and the 4th Cavalry near Clayton.

Buffalo was quite certain the crooked lawyer would still be there, ostensibly practising law but really waiting for news that Colorado had been located. And that was exactly what Buffalo planned to tell Maine. To make his story sound more plausible he would demand more money for the information. He could only guess what the crooked lawyer's reaction would be. But if he guessed correctly, he would then lead Maine into a trap from which the crooked lawyer would not be released until Colorado was long gone. In spite of what he had said to Sadie, he also had the semblance of a plan to prevent the showdown between his friend and Jake

Cobb. However, in that at least, time was not on his side.

Yet there was nothing Buffalo could do to speed up the uneventful trip. It was made even more tedious by the cavalry practice of riding for an hour, dismounting and then walking the horses, reins in hand, for the next hour. After which, the order to mount was given and the horses ridden for the following hour. Then, once again, the troops were ordered to dismount and to walk their horses until it was again time to remount. With only a short break at midday for cold rations, the process was repeated over and over again until dusk, at which time, camp was made.

Even then, the unfortunate troopers were not finished with their duties. While a couple of troopers lit a fire and cooked a meagre meal, the rest had to tend to the horses. Then, only half were permitted to eat while the others kept guard. After thirty minutes, the troops were ordered to change places. When everyone had finished eating, half the troops were detailed to keep watch while the others slept. Halfway through the night, their roles were reversed.

Buffalo despised the system. The troopers spent all their time following orders instead of scouring the passing countryside for signs of the Kwahadi. Scouting may have been his job but he couldn't cover all the ground on his own. Nevertheless, the routine was repeated without the slightest deviation every day.

After days of what seemed endless monotony, Buffalo persuaded the lieutenant to let him ride to an isolated settlement called Spring Falls to check if they had any news of hostile Indians. They hadn't. However, Buffalo had several friends in the settlement and over a hearty meal and some locally brewed beer he outlined his plan to entrap Maine. It wasn't difficult to enlist their co-operation, Colorado's support for the sodbuster and small time settlers was known throughout Texas.

Satisfied that the groundwork for his plans was in place, Buffalo returned to the troopers in time for their rendezvous with the 4th Cavalry. Desperate to make up for the time lost while escorting pacified tribes to their reservations, Colonel McKenzie and the 4th Cavalry set off after the Kwahadi without delay.

As Buffalo's services were no longer required by the cavalry, he rode back to Clayton. Buffalo had guessed Maine was still lodged in the town's only hotel. He also booked a room there and then ordered a bath, after which he made his way to the dining room. The crooked lawyer was already seated, about to start his evening meal.

Maine invited the scout to join him for dinner. But his apparently friendly greeting did nothing to dispel Buffalo's suspicions that the lawyer had hired Cobb to follow him. But he had to be sure before he put the second part of his plan in action.

'I've found your man,' he said as he sat down.

'Where?' asked the lawyer.

'Not so fast, Mr Maine. You promised me another hundred dollars for the information but I've had to lay out a lot of money for information that led me to him, so I want double.'

'No offence intended, Buffalo, it isn't that I doubt your word, but why hasn't Colorado come back with you to claim his inheritance?'

'A man with a price on his head is apt to be a mite cautious about riding into a strange town. But he will be at a settlement near here in a few days' time. I'm to take you there,' replied Buffalo.

'I don't like horse riding. I'm a lawyer, not a cowboy,' protested Maine.

'Don't worry. I'll go to the livery stables in the morning and pick out a docile horse for you.'

'But I can't just leave; I've got other business to which I must attend tomorrow.'

Buffalo had a shrewd idea what that other business was. If he was right, Maine would try to find out the name of the settlement in order to let Cobb know, and that was just what Buffalo wanted. He had given his word that he would not kill Maine but had made no such undertaking regarding Cobb. In town, in a one-to-one shoot-out with Cobb, Buffalo knew he stood no chance. But in Spring Falls, with his settler friends to back him up, he could dictate the terms of the showdown. It would be a fair fight, but with knives not with six-guns.

Maine interrupted Buffalo's thoughts. 'When I get to meet Colorado and only then, you will get an extra hundred dollars. But first, you must tell me where we are going. I'm obliged to keep my client up to date with the latest developments; after all he is paying my expenses and your finder's money.'

The lawyer's excuse finally confirmed Buffalo's suspicions. Yet he deliberately paused, hesitating just long enough to make his reply sound convincing.

'Seems fair enough to me, Mr Maine. The settlement is called Spring Falls but to get there in time for the rendezvous we have to leave by noon tomorrow.'

'Why Spring Falls?' asked the lawyer suspiciously.

'It's pretty isolated and its women are supposed to be real friendly. So where else would you go if you had a reward on your head and been on the trail for weeks?'

Maine seemed to be satisfied with Buffalo's answer. But that night the scout got to thinking. There must be an awful lot at stake for someone to pay the lawyer to go to so much trouble to find and kill Colorado. Yet that someone was taking a big chance. What was to stop Maine from blackmailing his client once he had come into his inheritance? Buffalo fell asleep trying to figure out that one.

Next day, they set out on schedule. Buffalo had selected a docile and broken-down hack for the lawyer to ride. Any westerner would have refused such a poor steed but the lawyer was city-born so knew no different. Nevertheless, in spite of the lawyer's protestations that he was no rider and the poor condition of his horse, they made steady progress throughout the rest of the day.

They camped at nightfall, if sleeping rough under the stars can be counted as camping. Buffalo slept soundly. However, unaccustomed to sleeping out in the open, the lawyer had a restless night and was in a thoroughly bad mood the following morning. So, next day, he failed to realize how much his hack was struggling to keep pace with Buffalo's steed.

They were still some miles from Spring Falls when they saw plumes of black smoke spiralling into the air. Buffalo urged his horse into a gallop; Maine's hack strove to follow but was soon left behind.

A scene of utter desolation met Buffalo as he entered what was left of Spring Falls. But it wasn't the burnt-out ruins that caused him to gasp in horror. Staked out on the grounds were the bodies of the inhabitants of the settlement, several of whom he had known for many years. Every male had been scalped. The dead women, although none had been scalped, were all naked. Buffalo didn't want to guess what unspeakable horrors they had suffered before the Indians had eventually dispatched them to their Maker.

Among the carnage were the bodies of several Indians. It was clear that the inhabitants of Spring Falls had fought valiantly before finally being overrun. Scattered all around the bodies were dozens of empty whiskey bottles. Indian war parties and whiskey were a very bad combination. Being liquored up undoubtedly accounted for the Indians' bestial treatment of the women.

For many years before he became a sheriff, Buffalo had been an Indian fighter. He had fought against the Chiricahua Apache (Cochise had been their chief) at Apache Pass; the Kiawah of East Texas and the Comanche sub-tribes of the Indian Territories. He had also had dealings with the Cheyenne and the Arapaho, yet the tribal markings of these dead Indians were completely unknown to him. Or were they? Long ago, had he not seen something quite similar?

Then it came to him: they were Oglala Sioux. But they belonged to the northern plains. And hadn't their chief, Red Cloud, once the scourge of the northern section of the US Cavalry, signed a peace treaty some years ago? So what was an Oglala war party doing in Comanche territory? Buffalo had no idea.

Had they simply jumped their reservation and were just on a drunken rampage, or were they on the way to join Quanah Parker? If so, they posed a new threat to McKenzie and the 4th. He was just trying to work out what to do about that when Maine arrived. Despite being unable to keep pace with Buffalo's mount, his hack was blowing hard.

The ghastly sight of the many corpses caused the lawyer to retch. When he recovered, he began to question Buffalo.

'Is Colorado among the dead?'

There was little point in Buffalo lying.

'Not as far as I can tell,' replied Buffalo.

'I suppose this was done by the savages McKenzie is chasing,' said Maine.

'Nope. Quanah doesn't leave his dead behind and these Indians,' Buffalo said, pointing at the dead Indians, 'are most likely Oglala Sioux not Comanche. Though what brought them so far south, I have no idea. But their presence here means big trouble.'

'And yet you led me to this terrible place. The sooner we get out of here, the better.'

'Hold on. This massacre only happened a few hours ago. Judging by the empty whiskey bottles lying around, the Indians responsible are probably dead drunk by now. I want to scout around and see if I can find out more about them and how many of them there are.'

'What does it matter?' asked Maine abruptly.

'However unlikely it may seem, if the Oglala join up with Quanah's Kwahadi, McKenzie and his 4th Cavalry may run into more than they can handle,' replied Buffalo.

'So? What's a few dead troopers to me?' snapped the lawyer. 'Let them get killed. Washington will send more.'

'But not for months. In the meantime,

Quanah and the Kwahadi will go on terrorizing ranchers and settlements.'

'Like I'm supposed to care. Look, I hired you to find Colorado not dead settlers, but if you get me back to safety you can have half of the fee I promised you!'

'No. In any case, your horse has to rest. It's just a stable hack not used to being ridden hard.'

'It can rest as long as it wants when we get back.'

'As you're paying me, all right. But let me just collect some feathers from the war bonnets of the dead Indians. Somebody might recognize them.'

'Fine, I'll wait for you along the trail.'

Before Buffalo could say it was not a good idea to split up again, Maine somewhat awkwardly remounted his horse and rode as swiftly out of Spring Falls as the hack could manage. But he didn't get far. From out of nowhere came a flight of arrows, several of which struck the lawyer. His horse bolted and a number of Indians, mounted on mustangs, gave chase. But not for long. The lawyer's horse had nothing left and soon stopped. It stopped because its rider was no longer able to spur the hack on. Maine's lifeless body fell to the ground.

There was nothing Buffalo could do to prevent the Indians scalping the dead man. So he remained hidden behind a smouldering building, his horse swiftly muzzled to prevent it from responding to the whinnies of the Indians' mustangs.

Perhaps eager to show off their coup to their fellow braves, the Indians soon left. But so broken down was Maine's hack, they left it behind.

As soon he was certain they were gone, Buffalo rode over to the body and searched the grisly remains. He was looking for any documentation relating to Colorado's inheritance. He found the papers and whistled with surprise as he quickly read them. The papers proved that Maine was not working for a client as he had claimed; he was Colorado's distant cousin and so next in line for his friend's inheritance should anything happen to him.

Buffalo also found a hundred dollars in Maine's wallet. He took the money and the papers, which he quickly stuffed into his saddle-bag. Then he returned to the ruined settlement and searched for anything else that might be useful. He found nothing except a couple of full whiskey bottles. These he also put in his saddle-bags.

He galloped away from Springs Falls, riding his steed until it was blowing hard. Then he slowed to little more than a canter and continued for another hour before finally dismounting and leading the horse on foot. Dusk came, but he continued on foot until the moon rose and gave enough light to ride by, if only at walking pace. A little after midnight, he stopped by a small waterhole to allow his horse to drink and rest. While the animal drank, he poured half the whiskey out of one of the bottles, topped it up with water and then drank it all in one go.

A lesser man might have become drunk, but not Buffalo. After refilling the whiskey bottle with water, he turned in for the night and rose just before dawn. His breakfast consisted of a slug of whiskey from the other bottle; then he saddled up and rode off just as the first rays of the sun lit the vast wilderness of the Texas Panhandle. Using the experience gained through many years of Indian fighting, he made very sure he left no tracks for the Indians to follow.

14

Colorado knew it was long past the time to move on. However, he had given his word that he would teach Helen and Petra how to handle a six-gun. So instead of leaving, he took Petra on to the range and showed her how best to hold a six-gun and how far to stand away from the target, then set up several rows of empty bean cans for her to aim at.

She didn't hit many. The recoil of the .45 calibre Peacemaker was too strong for her. Even after several days, she still missed far more cans than she hit; Helen was far worse, hitting only one can out of every five she shot at. However, she had a solution.

'My father had an old six-gun. I'm sure it was smaller and lighter than yours. It's still in the old trunk with the rest of his things; I could dig it out if you want.'

Her father's six-gun was an old,

hexagonally barrelled, .38 calibre Navy Colt, so-called because some versions had a naval scene depicted on their butt. However, the butt of this particular example was plain brown.

Unfortunately, unlike the new Peacemaker, which fired factory-made, shop-bought metallic cartridges, the Navy Colt fired a sort of make-it-yourself ammunition consisting of ball, powder and a percussion cap. Usually referred to as roll-your-own, it required a considerable amount of skill to make. So it was not surprising that it took Helen and Petra several more days before they could make bullets perfectly every time.

Once they got used to the Navy Colt, their aim improved and they were both able to consistently hit three bean cans out of every five shots. Even so, they both knew they needed to improve in order to satisfy Colorado.

Unfortunately, their training was brought to an end by an unexpected visitor. Extremely handsome, dressed completely in black and toting two pearl-handled six-guns, he rode a fine jet-black stallion at least the equal of Colorado's King. His Texas-style saddle was elaborately hand-stitched with what looked like gold thread. Clearly he was no ordinary drifter.

'Morning, ma'am,' he said courteously. 'Don't mean to trouble you, but I was on the trail nearby and I thought I heard shooting. Can I be of any assistance?'

'No thank you. It's just my man teaching my young nephew how to shoot straight.'

Of course, it was Petra shooting but Helen still felt compelled to protect her niece's true identity. There was something about this stranger that scared Helen even though neither his actions nor demeanour did anything to justify the feeling.

'In that case I'll be moving on, if I might be allowed to water my horse first.' The stranger smiled as he spoke and yet, to Helen, it seemed his eyes remained ice cold. They sent shivers of fear down her back but that didn't prevent her remembering her obligation as a host.

'Of course, the horse trough by the corral was only filled yesterday. The coffee is about to boil, won't you come in?'

'No, ma'am, but I'll take a cup outside if I may. That way, if your man returns, there can't be any unfortunate misunderstandings.'

Surprised at both his frankness and courtesy, Helen went into the ranch house and returned with the coffee. In the meantime, the stranger had dismounted and was busily seeing to his horse. Helen noticed he was especially careful not to let it drink too much at a time.

'If I'm not being too nosey, what brings you to these parts?' she asked.

'Not at all, ma'am. I was looking for a friend of mine called Buffalo. Then I heard there had been trouble at Adobe Wells, so I was on my way to see if there was anything I could do to help.'

'There was an Indian raid. I was there. Fortunately, the cavalry and some buffalo hunters drove the Indians off. Your friend Buffalo was there too but he left soon afterwards. He's scouting for the cavalry.'

'Before that, wasn't there a gunfight? A gunslinger called Frank Watson got himself killed, or so somebody told me.'

'Yes, he was my uncle. It was his son you heard shooting just now.'

'Mighty sorry to hear about the loss of your uncle. I heard tell he was no slouch with a six-gun, so the man who shot him must be pretty slick on the draw. Was it a man called Colorado by any chance?'

'I'm sorry, I was too upset to find out his name,' lied Helen. For some reason she couldn't explain she didn't want this courteous yet strangely sinister stranger to know anything about Colorado.

'Quite understandable, ma'am. Please accept my condolences and my apologies for asking. Well, as it seems everything is all right here, I'll be on my way.'

As the stranger mounted his jet-black horse, Helen asked one last question.

'May I know your name?'

'Why, of course ma'am. How unpardonably rude of me not to introduce myself. My name is Jake Cobb.'

The gunslinger smiled, mounted his horse and rode slowly away.

Cobb had been most courteous and yet his presence had sent shivers of fear down Helen's back. Instinctively, she knew that the gunslinger was the reason why Colorado had said he had to leave her ranch.

A little less than an hour after Jake Cobb left, Colorado and Petra returned from their shooting practice. However, to Helen, it seemed like an eternity, even though she had tried to keep herself busy preparing the evening meal.

Yet even when they returned, she felt she could not talk openly in front of her young niece. On the other hand, she also felt every moment Colorado remained lessened his chances of escaping.

'We've had a visitor,' she said, trying hard not to reveal the anxiety she felt.

'Anybody we know or was it just a drifter?' asked Petra.

'Never you mind who it was, young lady,' snapped Helen. 'Go and get cleaned up. You too, Colorado, dinner will be ready in a few minutes!'

It wasn't like Helen to be snappy, thought Colorado as he washed himself under the pump. Had the visitor upset her? However, he decided to wait until Petra had gone to bed before asking. But Petra was not prepared to let the matter rest so over dinner she brought up the subject again.

'Did the visitor have a name?' she asked.

'Jake Cobb. He said he was looking for the man who outdrew Petra's father,' Helen said breathlessly.

'Mr Colorado, you must leave at once,' interrupted Petra.

'Why?' asked Helen.

'Because Mr Buffalo told me that the man everyone called my father had called you out and you outdrew him in a fair gunfight.'

'Everyone called your father?' asked Colorado curiously.

'Before she died, Mama told me that my real father was killed in the Civil War.

189

His name was Peter, so she called me Petra after him.'

'Colorado wanted to tell you about the shooting as soon as he came back from Adobe Wells, but I wouldn't let him. I thought just knowing your father was dead was grief enough,' said Helen.

'Grief,' echoed Petra incredulously. 'Helen, I hated him for the way he treated my mama. Then there was the way he treated you. Even while he was here being especially nice to you, I knew he was seeing another woman and intended to go on seeing her after you married him.'

'How did you know about that?' asked Helen.

It was the first time Petra had used her aunt's first name yet Helen let it pass without comment.

'When he took me with him to get supplies for the ranch, I overheard him talking about you to Betsy. She said she didn't mind what he got up to with you so long as she got her cut from the sale of your ranch. I suppose they thought I wouldn't understand what they

190

meant, but I did. Everybody, except Mr Colorado, treats me like a child. But I'm not one anymore.'

'So it would seem,' said Colorado. 'So, for as long as I'm here, drop the 'Mr'; you've earned the right to call me Colorado.'

Petra blushed and flashed him that special smile only a girl growing into womanhood can give.

'You have to go. When will you leave?' Helen asked anxiously.

'As soon as I'm satisfied that you and Petra have left,' he replied.

'Why should we leave?' asked Helen.

'Because Cobb may return. I don't want you here when he finds I've left. So start packing.'

'But where shall we go?'

'To your friends in Indian Flats. They should have returned to the settlement by now. Even if Cobb knows of its existence I doubt if he will think it worth his while to follow you there, especially if he believes I've gone in the opposite direction. On my way, I'll call in at Adobe

Wells and let slip I'm leaving for Lincoln County.'

*　　*　　*

Later that night, after she had finished packing, Helen questioned Colorado.

'Where will you go?' she asked.

'I'm not sure. Like I said, I had intended to head for Lincoln County but I'd have to cross the Staked Plains. It would be just my luck to run into Quanah and the Kwahadi again.'

'So where else will you go?'

'South to Mexico. Best you don't know any more than that. But if Cobb does catch up with you again, tell him when I heard he had visited the ranch, I lit out in one big hurry.'

Helen sat silently for a while and then went to the kitchen to make coffee. When she returned her mood had changed.

'I suppose that this will be your last night at the homestead. Petra will miss you. Me too,' she said almost shyly.

'And I'll miss Petra very much and you even more.'

It was hard to tell whether Helen or Petra blushed more.

It was a sombre evening meal. Each was occupied with their own thoughts and what the morrow would bring. As soon as the meal was over, Petra excused herself and went to her room, saying she wanted to finish her packing. Helen went to help while Colorado surprised her by insisting on doing the washing up.

After the packing was finished and Petra had gone to bed, Helen again made coffee. She smiled as she put the coffee cups on to the table.

'I'll just go and check that Petra's asleep,' she said.

By the time Helen returned Colorado had finished his coffee, which was just as well for her appearance almost made him drop the cup. Not only was she completely naked but she had smothered her body in an erotic scented oil.

'It was given to me by Quanah when he was trying to persuade me to take up

193

with one of his braves. Apparently the Kwahadi girls wear it on their wedding night; it's supposed to make their brave go wild with passion.'

'I think your body would do that anyway,' said Colorado drily.

'Unfortunately, as the oil also badly stains clothes, I guess I'll just have to stand around like this until it dries. Unless you can think of anything better to do,' she said provocatively.

Colorado didn't need a second invitation and led her to her bedroom. They were still in bed next morning when Petra entered the bedroom carrying two mugs of coffee.

'Don't worry,' she said, adding cheekily, 'I can manage to load the luggage. Stay in bed while I make breakfast.'

'She has grown up,' said Helen. 'So let's make the most of our last few minutes together.'

Colorado agreed. In spite of their night of unrelenting passion, it still took them a considerable time to satisfy all their remaining desires.

15

Colorado waited until he was sure Helen and Petra were safely on their way to Indian Flats, then saddled up and left the ranch. However, he had done with running; he headed for Adobe Wells knowing that a showdown with Jake Cobb was inevitable.

He rode until dusk with only a few breaks to rest King. That night he camped under a starlit night sky and was on his way again at the crack of dawn arriving at Adobe Wells at noon. He booked a room, ordered a bath and then stabled his horse whilst it was being prepared.

'Jake Cobb's here and he's asking a lot of questions about you,' said the stable lad. 'But you're quite safe; nobody's told him you're living at the Blaine ranch.'

'Where's Cobb now?' asked Colorado.

'Shacked up with Betsy. So you could

slip away if you wanted. I won't tell him you've been here.'

'No. I've done with running. So, if you see him, you can tell him I'm looking for him.'

After a gloriously hot bath, a change of clothes and a decent meal, Colorado made his way to the saloon. As usual, it was almost empty. Nevertheless, the atmosphere was extremely tense, suggesting that Cobb was not far away.

Colorado's assumption was correct. He ordered a beer but before he could pay for it an educated voice politely interrupted him.

'Barkeeper, if the gentleman has no objections to drinking with me, I'd like to buy him that drink and perhaps a whiskey chaser to go with it. But none of the slop you serve the drunks, only your best whiskey for my friend.'

Colorado turned round. Less than ten paces in front of him was a man dressed completely in black. Even if his unusually macabre-coloured clothing didn't identify him, the expensive pearl handles of two six-guns protruding from holsters on either side of his waist belt did.

'I have no objections at all,' said Colorado as he positioned his right hand over his Peacemaker.

'Easy friend,' said Cobb. 'There will be no gunplay started by me tonight, you have my word. I just want a civilized drink between two gentlemen of the road. Shall we find a table where we can talk?'

'That's fine by me,' said Colorado and followed Cobb across the saloon to a table in a quiet corner of the saloon.

Not that anywhere in the saloon was noisy. Fearful of what they saw as an inevitable gunfight, most of its few patrons had already made a hasty exit. The rest stood motionless and silent, intrigued by the situation being played out before their eyes.

'A good friend told me you've been looking for me,' said Colorado as an extremely nervous-looking barkeeper brought over their drinks.

Cobb lifted his glass and smiled. Yet there was little warmth in his ice-blue eyes.

'I wish you well, if not a long life,' he said as he sipped his beer. He held the glass in his right hand and kept his left hand in plain sight on the table.

'And I wish that circumstances between us were different so I could wish you both,' replied Colorado.

'Under the circumstances, that's extremely magnanimous of you,' said Cobb. 'However, I am afraid your growing reputation with a six-gun has made this meeting inevitable. And yes, I followed Buffalo Brown for several weeks believing he was also looking for you. But instead, he joined a group of professional buffalo hunters. I watched from a distance and he seemed to be doing so well that I thought he had given up looking for you. He hadn't, of course, and while he was supposedly hunting buffalo he gave me the slip. Took me some time to pick up his trail again. But as you see, I eventually found you.'

'I really don't understand why you've gone to so much trouble,' said Colorado.

'I assure you it's been no trouble. I felt that we ought to have this little chat,' said Cobb. 'But where is your friend, Buffalo? I expected him to be here. To save any possible future unpleasantness between us, I would have liked to explain the situation to him as well.'

'He's on a temporary assignment, a scouting mission for the cavalry.'

'So I've heard, but it's most unfortunate. I met him once and he struck me as being an honourable man. After our set to I'm afraid he will probably think it's his duty to call me out. As he's never claimed to be a match for me, there's little point in me killing him.'

'But I've never claimed I'm faster than you,' protested Colorado.

'Unfortunately, that's not the point,' replied Cobb. 'You see, more and more people think you might be, so I have to prove them wrong. There's nothing personal in it. I have to go on proving I'm the fastest gun in Texas. It's just the way I am.'

'So when is this showdown to be?' asked Colorado.

'I know you won't run. So there's no real hurry. Shall we say an hour before noon, a week today? That should also be enough time for news of our showdown to spread and people to come and watch us and hopefully Buffalo will return before then. If he does, please do your best to dissuade him from calling me out after our showdown.'

'Very well,' agreed Colorado as he sipped the last of his beer.

'Good. This has been a most satisfactory conversation. For my part, I promise you a quick and painless end.'

It was a very strange week. News of the shoot-out spread like wildfire but most people, fearful the outcome of the shoot-out would not favour Colorado, were too embarrassed to speak to him. Indeed, Jake Cobb, when he was not involved with Betsy, was the only person prepared to have a drink with him. Sadie, on the other hand, did share a couple of evening meals with him. But, nothing else. It was quite clear she had become enraptured with Buffalo and wanted to know everything about him.

However, the man himself arrived a few days later with the news of the demise of Maine and that the crooked lawyer had been next in line for Colorado's inheritance. So, apart from Cobb, the way was clear for Colorado to return east.

'Why don't you hit the trail?' asked Buffalo that evening as they shared a beer or two. 'If you change your appearance a bit and use your real name, how's Cobb going to trace you back to Richmond?'

'I've given my word to Cobb that I won't run,' replied Colorado.

There seemed to be nothing Buffalo could say to change Colorado's mind. Yet he had to try.

'I had a scheme to take care of Cobb but the Indian raid on Spring Falls put paid to it. Take my word for it, against Cobb you don't stand a chance, nobody does. Take the money I earned hunting buffalo and hit the trail. The buffalo will be back for at least one more year so I'll more than make up the money then.'

Of course, Colorado refused the offer. There was nothing more to be said.

The next day, the eve of the showdown, seemed endless. Yet evening eventually arrived and with it, a knock on Colorado's bedroom door. It was the stable lad with a note from Cobb.

No one should be alone on their last night. I have Betsy to keep me company, so you should have someone as well. Please accept what follows this note with my compliments. ...'

The stable lad indicated that no reply was expected and then left. But what did Cobb mean? Half an hour later there came another knock on the bedroom door. Colorado opened it and the answer to Cobb's riddle stood before him.

It was Ami, Sadie's friend. She wore a red dress, cut very low. Indeed, it made the revealing dresses Sadie used to wear in the saloon seem quite respectable.

'Aren't you going to ask me why I'm here?' she asked.

'Yes, of course,' stammered Colorado. 'To what do I owe this unexpected pleasure?'

She followed him in and came straight to the point.

'Mr Cobb says you shouldn't be alone tonight. You probably think I'm a poor substitute for Sadie, but if you come to my room tonight I'll do my best to change your mind.'

She was right. Ami wouldn't have been his choice, although she was young and quite attractive. Yet, whatever the outcome of tomorrow's showdown, it was unlikely he would ever see Helen again. So he followed Ami to the saloon and then up to her, well, French-style boudoir was a better description than merely bedroom.

Ami's actions were far more than just professional and as she promised, she did change his mind. Her passion and expertise in love-making made Sadie seem like a novice. Nevertheless, no matter how willing and wild she became, Ami was not Helen and no matter how he tried, Colorado could not quite manage to put her out of his mind.

During a lull in their night's passion, something Buffalo had said about Cobb's shoot-out in Waynoka with the gunman, Jed Blake, flashed unbidden into his head. However, the needs of the insatiable Ami gave him little chance to dwell on it.

Although it was her room, she left with the coming of dawn. He slept on but an hour later Ami was back and with her came breakfast, again provided by courtesy of Jake Cobb. It was a magnificent affair: a large tee-bone steak topped with two fried eggs and lashings of fried onions. They ate in silence and over what Cobb and Ami obviously thought would be Colorado's last meal, he worked out a plan for the shoot-out based on the idea that had come to him during the night. With Buffalo's help and a very large slice of luck he might yet best Cobb and still manage to shed the image of being *the fastest gun in Texas*.

16

Five minutes before eleven, Colorado stepped on to the street. He was surprised to see there were as many as seventy or even eighty people safely positioned between the three main buildings of Adobe Wells. No doubt Jake Cobb would be pleased with the turnout. Not that Colorado minded; he had his own reasons for wanting a lot of witnesses.

Almost at the same moment, Jake Cobb stepped out of the saloon and started to walk, very slowly, towards Colorado. From that moment, Colorado's attention was fully focused on the gunslinger. Otherwise, he might have noticed that in the crowd was a horrified Helen. Petra was with her and she too was very distressed. However, as she was again dressed as a boy, she tried hard to hold back her tears.

Helen had known nothing about the shoot-out but, bored of sitting and doing nothing at Indian Flats, she had come to Adobe Wells partly to stock up on supplies but mainly to see if Colorado was still in the settlement. She didn't really expect him to still be there but if he was she hoped ... well she wasn't quite sure what she hoped.

Of course, she soon found out that Colorado was indeed in Adobe Wells; the showdown with Cobb was the talk of the little settlement. In the hope of talking Colorado out of the gunfight she tried desperately to find him but failed. Perhaps that was just as well for Colorado was breakfasting with Ami in her French-style boudoir.

So, horrified, Helen could only wait until the showdown. Worse still, there was nothing she could do to prevent Petra watching the action too. Full of dread, Helen felt even more helpless than when Colorado had chosen to fight Quanah's top brave.

When they were just ten paces apart, Cobb stopped. A kind of madness blazed from his eyes as he carefully removed a silver fob watch from his waistcoat and flipped the case lid open. Yet he spoke rationally enough.

'When the case is open, it chimes the hours. If you're agreeable, I'll put it on the ground and we draw as it strikes for the eleventh time.'

Colorado nodded his approval. There wasn't long to wait. The watch began to chime. Carefully, he counted down the chimes. The crowd held their breath: eight, nine, ten; Helen bit back a scream — eleven: then, feet apart to ensure an accurate shot, Colorado swayed his head to one side and in the same instant, drew.

The outlaw was faster than a flash of lightning. Nevertheless, as his finger squeezed the trigger, the world exploded around him. As he felt himself falling he saw Cobb stagger. Colorado's last thought as the black cloak of unconsciousness engulfed him was that Cobb had kept his word; this death didn't hurt.

Both six-guns drawn and fired, Cobb regained his balance and stood motionless; a smile of triumph crossed his face as he gazed at Colorado's prostrate body.

'I am still the fastest gun in Texas!' he cried to the crowd. But as deep red blood began to stain his black shirt, his knees buckled and he pitched forward.

At first, the crowd were too stunned to move. However, Buffalo rushed forward and stooped to examine Colorado. But only briefly. He then walked over to the fallen Cobb and turned his body over with his foot.

A smile had frozen on the gunfighter's face even though Colorado's bullet had hit him full in the chest. That he had remained on his feet after he had been hit was quite beyond Buffalo's comprehension. To Helen's absolute horror, Buffalo then shook his head, indicating to the crowd that both protagonists were dead. Too distraught to think clearly, she started to move towards Colorado's body, but found herself restrained by a firm pair of female arms.

'It will do no good,' said Sadie firmly. 'Best get Petra away from the bodies.'

She led a sobbing Helen away. Yet Petra didn't cry. Instead, she looked intently at the prostrate body of Colorado and then at Cobb's. For the merest moment a smile flickered across her face and then it was gone as she too turned away. Then, in spite of her tender years, she followed Helen and Sadie into the saloon.

One grave had already been prepared in Boot Hill, a small area in the main cemetery reserved for those who had died fighting 'with their boots on'. The heat of a hot Texas summer dictated rapid burial and it took place almost as soon as the second grave had been dug. The coffins were buried with little ceremony, although many of the crowd, including a distraught Helen, stopped to watch it.

Immediately afterwards, two hastily constructed wooden crosses were placed over the graves. One carried the epitaph, *Jake Cobb, the fastest gun in Texas* and on the other was engraved just one word, *Colorado.*

Helen desperately wanted to leave but she still had to get supplies, the main reason for her trip to Adobe Wells. Unfortunately, the store was full to over-flowing with would-be customers, many of the people who had really come to witness. Most of them were now doing so before returning to their homes. So by the time Helen was served and the supplies loaded, it was almost dark and far too late to start out for her little ranch.

Sadie came to the rescue; she let Helen and Petra stay in her room above the sa-loon. Where Sadie slept that night, Helen didn't ask, although she was certain that wherever it was she wasn't alone; there was also no sign of Buffalo.

They set out next day. Helen was still bitterly distraught, but chided herself for letting her feelings overwhelm her. Since she had never expected to see Colorado again, what difference did his death make? Yet it did, and horribly so. Strangely, Petra seemed quite calm.

Once well clear of Adobe Wells, neither Helen nor Petra had any fears of camping overnight. Nevertheless, Helen kept her father's old Navy Colt, uncocked but fully loaded, by her side.

The old wagon was heavily overloaded and hard going for its horses, unsuited as they were for pulling wagons. As a result the horses needed frequent rest periods and that made for a very slow journey. So slow, they were forced to pull well off the trail and camp for a second night. Worn out by grief and the arduous task of driving a team of horses untrained for wagon work, Helen slept soundly all through the night and well beyond dawn.

Not so for Petra. For most of the night, holding the old six-gun, she kept guard over Helen. In any event, there was no need, for the night passed by without incident. However, just before Helen awoke, Petra heard the sound of a well-shod horse coming slowly down the trail from Adobe Wells.

She blessed at least one of the many lessons Colorado had taught her. With boyish athleticism, she raced to the horses and quickly muzzled them to prevent them neighing a greeting to the passing horse.

Fortunately, Helen had chosen the camp site well. Both wagon and horses had been hidden behind a clump of stubby cottonwoods well out of sight of the trail. So the rider failed to notice them. Unfortunately, Petra was unable to see him. Not that it mattered for now he had passed by, she was almost certain of his identity.

It was another hour before Helen awoke to the delightful smell of breakfast. Petra was cooking bacon and eggs. She had not only gathered firewood but had also managed to light it, courtesy of another one of Colorado's lessons.

Helen was ashamed that she had slept through the night leaving Petra to guard the camp. Yet she was also proud of Petra and her resourcefulness. At that moment she silently vowed that whatever else the future held, she would not be parted from her protégée until such time as Petra decided to marry.

Breakfast over, whilst Helen doused the fire Petra harnessed the horses.

Progress remained slow and it was not until mid-afternoon that they eventually reached home.

Much to Helen's surprise, although there was no other horse in sight, smoke coming from its chimney indicated there was somebody inside the ranch. Yet except for the smell of cooking emanating from the kitchen, there was no greeting.

Helen looked askance at Petra. However, far from being alarmed, she just smiled.

'Petra, stay in the wagon,' Helen ordered.

Helen retrieved her Navy Colt, cocked it and then climbed down from the wagon. In spite of the clatter of noisy arrival, no one came out to greet them. Heart beating wildly, Helen entered her little ranch house.

'Who's there?' she asked.

'Shan't be a second,' came a muffled voice from the kitchen.

Determined to find out who dared to cook in her house, Helen marched into the kitchen just as its occupant was coming out. They collided. She would have been knocked off her feet if a pair of strong arms had not caught hold of her and then grabbed the old Navy Colt from her outstretched hand.

She looked up into the stranger's face. Except he was no stranger. She gasped in amazement and then fainted.

*   *   *

As she came to her senses, she found she was sitting in her favourite armchair.

'Are you all right? You gave me quite a scare!' said a familiar voice. It was Colorado. Under his Stetson she could see his head was heavily bandaged.

'Is it really you? I thought you were dead,' she gasped.

'Only the good die young,' he said with a smile.

A mixture of anger and relief surged through her. She stood up and advanced towards him, eyes blazing.

'Colorado! You mean to say you were just play-acting all the time! Have you any idea what I've been going through?' she said furiously.

'Well, as you can see, I wasn't entirely play-acting,' said Colorado, pointing to his bandaged head.

'What really happened?'

'Buffalo once said that Cobb always aimed to hit his opponent between his eyes. So, just before I drew I swayed slightly and moved my head to one side. Even so, he was too fast for me. Just as I fired, one of his bullets grazed my temple. If I hadn't moved, it would have hit me between the eyes. As it was, it only knocked me out.'

'And Cobb?'

'Dead. I don't mean to be morbid, but I always aim for the heart and so far I haven't missed.'

'So who is in your coffin?'

'Nobody. As part of our plan Buffalo had already persuaded the undertaker to fill it with stones.'

'Why didn't you tell me you were going after Cobb?' asked Helen crossly.

'So you wouldn't worry. I wasn't sure I'd outdraw Cobb.'

'So why have you come back? You said were going to New Mexico.'

'No need. But it's a long story. Let me finish preparing dinner and perhaps you had better prepare Petra for my sudden reappearance. When I didn't pass you on the road I though you must have taken a different trail.'

'No need to prepare me. I'd already guessed you weren't dead and you did pass us on the trail. We were camped behind a thicket of cottonwoods and I'd muzzled the horses so nobody riding past would hear them call out,' said Petra. Tired of waiting outside, she had quietly come inside and had overheard everything.

'I'm impressed by your resourcefulness,' said Colorado, smiling broadly.

Petra blushed deeply, too embarrassed by the generous compliment to speak. Inwardly, she was delighted.

Over dinner, Colorado began to relate his story.

'You see, apart from Buffalo, the only man who knew my real name was a lawyer called Maine. It seems my uncle has passed away. As a boy I was always his favourite nephew and, as his wife died before they had any children, he left me his plantation. It's in Virginia. It seems my uncle's wife was Maine's aunt and as she is also dead, Maine would have been next in line for my inheritance if I had been killed. So he hired an old friend of mine called Buffalo to find me and then arranged for Jake Cobb to follow him hoping Cobb would then kill me. But a war party of Indians killed Maine at a place called Spring Falls. So I'm free to go back to Richmond and claim my inheritance.'

'What about your friend Buffalo, will he go back to hunting?'

'No. There's a large timber mill on my plantation and a good-sized family house goes with it. I've persuaded him to come back with me and run the timber side of the plantation. But first he wanted to clear up some personal business in Adobe

Wells. When I heard the wagon I thought he had arrived.'

'Why would Buffalo be driving a wagon?' asked Helen.

'Because he hoped to bring someone with him.'

'A companion? Who would that be?' asked Petra, filled with curiosity.

'Wait and see,' replied Colorado mysteriously.

The wait was not long. They had barely finished eating when a chuck wagon rattled into the yard. It was pulled by no less than six sturdy horses. Driving it was Buffalo and seated on the passenger seat was Sadie.

After the reunion, Buffalo went to tend the horses. Although she could not offer any practical help, Sadie went with him.

'I've got so used to calling you Colorado. What's your proper name?' asked Helen.

'A fair question.' Colorado smiled as he continued. 'Yet I'm afraid you may think it's too much trouble to find out the answer.'

'I don't understand. What do you mean?'

'I mean to find out my real name you're going to have to leave your little ranch, marry me and come with me to Virginia to claim my inheritance. Of course Petra must come too. We could officially adopt her if she wishes.'

'I'd better start packing,' said Petra, grinning from ear to ear. 'As I said, I thought you weren't dead. After the shoot-out I looked closely at your body and saw you were still breathing. I'm sorry I didn't tell you, Helen, but if I had then anybody looking at you would have seen your relief and guessed Colorado was only shamming.'

'So why didn't you tell me on the way back home? Helen asked angrily.

'I wasn't sure whether Colorado would come back to the ranch or ride on to New Mexico and I didn't want you disappointed again.'

Helen's eyes were full of tears as she hugged Petra but they were tears of joy.

Colorado's eyes were fixed only on Helen.

'Well, Helen, what's it to be? Will you be my wife and come with me to Virginia?'

'The wagon's still full of supplies. We could transfer most of them to the chuck wagon,' Helen said happily.

'I think you two need some privacy,' said Petra, again showing she was worldly wise beyond her age. 'So while Buffalo is still tending to the horses, I'll begin to transfer our provisions into the chuck wagon. With Sadie's help we might get enough done tonight to start for Virginia tomorrow, if that's you want.'

Helen's smile was answer enough for Colorado.

17

Early next morning, Colorado and Buffalo completed transferring the rest of the provisions to the chuck wagon. While Helen cooked breakfast, Petra and Sadie filled the chuck wagon with two large water barrels. The first stop on the long road to Virginia was Clayton and every drop of water would be needed on that arid trail, especially for the horses.

Helen's wagon was to be used as sleeping quarters for the women and young Petra while the men took it in turns to keep watch at night. During the long journey to Clayton, Helen and Petra took it in turns to drive her wagon. Freed from most of its load, Helen's two horses managed to keep up with the heavily loaded chuck wagon quite easily. While Buffalo scouted ahead and sometimes behind to check if they were being followed, Colorado drove the chuck wagon. Although he initially found the six-horse team difficult to manage, he soon mastered the art.

The long trek back to Clayton was completely uneventful. As the former sheriff of the town, Buffalo was the obvious man to order the rooms they needed to stay in. So he and the women went to the hotel while Colorado and Petra drove the wagons to the stables to arrange for them to be stored and the horses to be stabled — for however long was needed to arrange the joint weddings and then for the official adoption of Petra by Helen and Colorado to be arranged.

However, when Colorado and Petra reached the stable, Colorado was unexpectedly reunited with a young friend whose parting words, *'When I grow up, I want to be just like you,'* he had never quite forgotten.

Working in Clayton's only stable was young Joe. All the youngster had to do to earn the thousand-dollar bounty on Colorado's head was to report the outlaw to the sheriff.

He did not do so. Instead, he competently handled the stabling of the horses, eight in all, and placed the easily identifiable King in one of the least visible stalls at the rear of the stable. As he did so, Colorado questioned him.

'What happened to you?' he asked.

'Just after you left, my ma died. The deputy was still out looking for you, but when the sheriff returned from Indian Flats he started to make enquiries about your escape and they led him straight to me. Luckily he couldn't prove I was the one who had tipped you off, but as I'd searched the saloons trying to find you, sooner or later he was sure to find out. I thought about taking a horse and following after you but, although I practised a bit, I can't shoot straight. Besides, they hang people for horse stealing, don't they?'

'Yes, but you haven't explained why you came to Clayton,' said Colorado.

'Like I said, the sheriff was bound to discover I'd been asking around for you. But his deputy sheriff and his normal posse were still out chasing you so I thought if I slipped out of Evington quietly and without causing any trouble, the sheriff might think it was too much trouble to chase me, at least until his regular posse returned.'

'As you're here it must have worked.'

'Yes, I took the money owed to me, an old Bowie knife that had been thrown away and a water canteen. After drinking my fill of water twice over, I waited for nightfall and set out.'

'You walked all the way! But there's no direct trail across the Panhandle to Clayton as far as I know,' exclaimed Colorado.

'Even if there had been, I wouldn't have dared use it.'

'But how did you find your way?' asked an equally astounded Petra.

'Rested during the day. I knew Clayton was almost due north so used the stars to guide me. After a few days things were getting a bit desperate, but then I got lucky and hit a back trail. After a day on it I was picked up by a wagon and its folks took me all the way to Clayton. Then I had another piece of luck. The deputy sheriff and his posse had already visited Clayton and were long gone. I figured they wouldn't be back, so I got a job at the stable. But don't worry, Mr Colorado; I won't give you away. Your secret is safe with me.'

'I believe you,' said Petra, her eyes full of admiration.

Over dinner that night, they discussed young Joe.

'He can't be left here,' said Buffalo. 'Sooner or later, he might let slip that the famous outlaw Colorado got married here. The sheriff will then beat out of him that we intended to settle down in Virginia and send for a bounty hunter or two. It wouldn't be that difficult for them to track our two wagons and Colorado's palomino all the way to Richmond.'

'But only if we get married. We must postpone it until we find a town where nobody knows you,' said Helen tearfully.

'Helen, getting married wouldn't make any difference,' said Colorado gently.

'If it ever gets out that I've been here and am heading eastwards in a party of five, bounty hunters will follow after us. Remember, there's a reward of one thousand dollars for my capture.'

'The only one who can identify you is young Joe. What if I scare him a bit? I could tell him as the ex-sheriff of Clayton it's my duty to inform the sheriff of Evington that Joe's living in Clayton. Then, one of you could slip him a hundred dollars and a good horse. I've got the money for both. Then, with a little more pressure, he might just head out west.'

'And then what? He'd probably become an outlaw, and that's something I don't want on my conscience,' said Colorado bitterly.

'Well, has anybody else got a better idea?' asked Buffalo.

'We could take him with us. There must be work he could do on the plantation,' said Petra.

For some considerable time they argued over Petra's suggestion but failed to reach agreement. So they decided to vote on it. Colorado and Helen voted in favour of her idea but Buffalo preferred his own plan. Of course, Sadie sided with Buffalo. So they were no further forward. Then Sadie had an idea.

'Let Petra have the deciding vote,' she said.

'Why not. It was her idea,' said Helen.

'She's earned the right and, apart from me, she's the only other one of us that has actually met Joe,' said Colorado.

Buffalo nodded his agreement.

Her face scarlet with embarrassment at the responsibility given to her, Petra paused for thought and then said, 'If he wants to, it would be better if he came with us. Even if he goes west he could still let slip what he knows about my dad.' She blushed even deeper as she looked at Colorado.

So it was agreed and next morning Colorado and Petra paid another visit to the stable. Colorado put both plans to Joe but the lad didn't give Buffalo's plan a moment's thought. Never taking his eyes off Petra, who was wearing her prettiest dress, he immediately agreed to join them on their way to Virginia.

A few days later, Colorado and Helen and Buffalo and Sadie got married in a joint ceremony. Petra was bridesmaid. The following day the local circuit judge declared Petra to be the legally adopted daughter of Helen and Colorado and for an additional fifty dollars — provided by Buffalo — issued a certificate to prove it. Then, they travelled to Richmond, the city in which Colorado had grown up. Consequently, there were few problems in claiming his inheritance.

The massive plantation proved to be highly prosperous. Fortunately, it already had a very good manager who was only too happy to show Colorado the ropes. However, even when he had learnt how to run the plantation, Colorado insisted the manager stayed on and gave him a handsome rise in recognition of all the good work he had done.

Helen took a little time to get used to being the mistress of a house that had ten bedrooms, not including those in the attic set aside for the servants. But it was not long before she began to take her turn giving some of the grandest balls in the area.

Much to his surprise, Buffalo took to running the sawmill as if he had been in the business all his life. The ex-Indian fighter and former buffalo hunter also proved to be an astute businessman and profits soon began to increase.

During the long journey from Clayton to Richmond, Buffalo took a real shine to Joe. So once Buffalo had settled in at the sawmill he promised Joe a key role in its running, but not before the lad had worked his way through all its departments.

Petra settled to southern ways as if she had been born to them. However, she did retain some of her old Texas ways. When offered a pony for her fifteenth birthday she declined and opted for a real Texas mustang. As she grew older she developed into a real beauty and was courted by almost all the rich young men of Richmond. Typically, she rejected them all. Instead, much to Colorado's amusement, she relentlessly pursued Joe, and when he became under-manager of the sawmill they were married.

Epilogue

In Virginia, no one had any reason to connect the owner of a highly successful plantation with the notorious outlaw called Colorado, and in Texas other desperadoes soon caught the attention of the bounty hunters. However, the Lone Star State never forgot the chief of the Kwahadi Comanche, Quanah Parker.

No matter how hard Colonel McKenzie and the 4th Cavalry tried, they could not best the Kwahadi and their great leader, and the Indians continued to terrorize the whole of west Texas. Then came a particularly harsh winter.

In the spring of the following year, Colonel McKenzie, on behalf of the United States government, offered the Kwahadi a truce. There was also the promise that there would be no recriminations if he led his followers to a large reservation in the Indian territories especially set aside for them.

Colonel McKenzie had little hope that the offer would be accepted. So he was astounded when, under the flag of truce, Quanah led his braves into the camp of the 4th Cavalry and then surrendered, giving his word that never again would the Kwahadi take up arms against the white man. It was a promise never broken.

Colonel McKenzie, also a man of his word, led the troops which escorted the Kwahadi to their reservation. Unlike most other such treks during which the Indians were humiliated by being forced to give up their horses and proceed on foot, the Kwahadi were allowed to ride in style and keep all their possessions. McKenzie also saw to it that Quanah Parker was treated with respect.

At first, times on the reservation were hard for the Kwahadi. Food and blankets promised under the terms of the truce were often late and usually insufficient.

Then, Quanah was allowed off the reservation to seek his white mother. He arrived at the Parker family's home only to find she had died from a fever some time before. Quanah was surprisingly well received by his estranged family and during his stay, he learnt to speak English. By the time he returned to the reservation he was fully conversant with the ways of the white man.

So much so, that on behalf of his people, he began to exact a toll from the many herds driven from Texas across the Indian territories to the great railhead towns such as Dodge or Wichita. Although at first not every herd paid in full, most contributed something. Initially, the money obtained was used to buy much-needed food and blankets for his people.

Most trail bosses soon began to realize there were real benefits from paying the toll. The Kwahadi not only helped return strays but kept all other Indians at bay. More and more trail drivers paid up. Consequently the Kwahadi began to prosper, but that prosperity weakened when the reservation was threatened by droves of white settlers from the east.

Instead of resorting to force, Quanah tried diplomacy and received strong support from a powerful if unlikely source: many of the ranch owners he had once terrorized offered their support for the Kwahadi cause. Of course, in doing so they were also helping themselves. If the settlers could be kept off the Comanche reservation then maybe they could also be kept away from the open ranges of the western Panhandle.

So together, the ranchers and Quanah Parker mounted a powerful lobby which took them right to the very seat of government in Washington D.C. There, Quanah's eloquence won the day. Further settlements were not only barred from the reservation but also from most of the north-west ranges of the Texas Panhandle. However, there was one battle Quanah could not win: the slaughter of the buffalo continued until they were all but extinct.

In gratitude for Quanah's achievement, Burdett, one of the biggest and richest ranch owners in Texas, built Quanah a magnificent ranch house large enough to accommodate all twenty-five of his wives and their many children.

In later life a wealthy man, Quanah became a fully-fledged judge. He was noted for dispensing justice fairly, irrespective of race, colour or gender. Although it was often said that his justice was a mixture of white and Indian law, few had cause to complain.

Although he did nothing to stop the Kwahadi adopting Christianity, Quanah remained true to the traditions of the Kwahadi Comanche all his life. Yet when he died of old age, his epitaph, fully endorsed by many of the great Texas ranches he had once terrorized, read; *Quanah Parker, a true son of Texas.*

The Fastest Gun in Texas is a work of fiction, but some of the characters were actual people.

Quanah Parker was, of course, a real Kwahadi-Comanche chief. Except for his relationship to my fictitious heroine, Helen, everything else attributed to him actually happened. However, I have not attempted to translate his Comanche name, for in English it is apparently 'Fragrant'.

There is a more serious problem in translating the name of Isa-Tai, also a real person, since there appear to be differing interpretations, none of which ought to appear in print. Two other characters were also real: Colonel McKenzie and Bull Bear, chief of the Kwahadi-Comanche.

In conclusion, the battle at Adobe Wells (actually named Adobe Walls) was also real, although I have added cavalry troopers and settlers to the action. In reality, twenty-seven buffalo and one woman repelled seven hundred armed Indians.

Edwin Derek

We do hope that you have enjoyed reading this large print book.

Did you know that all of our titles are available for purchase?

We publish a wide range of high quality large print books including:
Romances, Mysteries, Classics
General Fiction
Non Fiction and Westerns

Special interest titles available in large print are:
The Little Oxford Dictionary
Music Book, Song Book
Hymn Book, Service Book

Also available from us courtesy of Oxford University Press:
Young Readers' Dictionary
(large print edition)
Young Readers' Thesaurus
(large print edition)

For further information or a free brochure, please contact us at:
Ulverscroft Large Print Books Ltd.,
The Green, Bradgate Road, Anstey,
Leicester, LE7 7FU, England.
Tel: (00 44) 0116 236 4325
Fax: (00 44) 0116 234 0205

Other titles in the
Linford Western Library:

THE BROKEN TRAIL

Alexander Frew

After a gang of robbers tries to kill him on the trail to Coker, Cody is lost and wounded. When he finally arrives in town, the corrupt sheriff blames him for the murder of a prominent citizen, who was slain by the same gang. Cody vows that he will unleash death and destruction on the men who embroiled him in this fight — but he has been thrown into a tiny cell, falsely identified by the widow of the dead man, and today, without trial, he must hang . . .

DEAD MAN RIVER

Tyler Hatch

At first, it seemed to Dave Brent like a wonderful solution to his troubles: exchange identities with the dead man he found floating in the river, and that should be the last he'd hear of the Vandemanns, who wanted his blood. But the dead man was more popular than Dave reckoned — and a lot of men want to find the one now using his name. If they catch him, they intend to offer him a choice of deaths — by torture or a quick bullet. Dave isn't keen on either option . . .

BAD NIGHT AT THE CRAZY BULL

John Dyson

After a night of drinking at the Crazy Bull Hotel, Glen Stone wakes up to find himself in bed with a saloon girl who informs him that they have been married. When Glen returns with her to his ranch, he must deal with her refusal to do her share of the work, the assorted unsavoury characters her presence attracts, and the wrath of his long-time intended and her father. Will the arrival of horse preacher Repentance Rathbone restore harmony to the lives of the Wyoming ranchers?

CHILCOT'S REDEMPTION

Ethan Harker

Brook Chilcot's career as a sheriff ended after a disastrous shootout, and he is in no hurry to forgo his alcoholic haze. But when a young man wishing to be taught how to shoot convinces him to leave retirement, Brook returns to the town of Grafton's Peak, where he must deal with new faces and old enemies. As the son of an outlaw he killed many years ago arrives to confront him, Chilcot is given the chance to make up for his errors in the past. Will he take it?

KNIGHTS OF THE BAR 10

Boyd Cassidy

When Gene Adams and his riders of the Bar 10 arrive in the town of McCoy with their prime steers, they find the pens filled with Circle O and Lazy J stock, leaving less cash for their beeves. But corrupt cattle agent Roscoe Martin has hired a gunfighter to rob the weary Circle O and Lazy J boys of their money on their way home. Adams and his men saddle up in a bid to warn their rivals. They are no longer just cowboys: they are the Knights of the Bar 10.